Secrets Not Meant to be Kept

I glance up, suddenly aware that Daddy is standing in the doorway. Becky's back is to him. The look on his face is one of shock and horror. I give him the slightest of nods to stop him from intruding and go on with my questions. I am cold and sick with knowing, even though I knew the answers long before I asked the questions.

When I glance up to the doorway again, Daddy is leaning against the frame. One arm shields his eyes, and his body is shaking with silent sobs.

Also available in Lions Tracks

Gloria D. Miklowitz

Secrets Not Meant to be Kept

COLLINS

LIONS · TRACKS

First published in the USA by Delacorte Press in 1987
First published in Great Britain in Lions Tracks in 1989

Lions Tracks is an imprint of
the Children's Division, part of
the Collins Publishing Group,
8 Grafton Street, London W1X 3LA

Copyright © 1987 by Gloria D. Miklowitz

Printed and bound in Great Britain by
William Collins Sons & Co. Ltd, Glasgow

For David and Paul,
always with love

Chapter 1

I'll let you feed the rabbits . . . if . . .

Hairbrush poised halfway to my head I stare at my image in the mirror. Eyes dark, secretive, perhaps even frightened.

Weird.

It's the third time this week the odd phrase has jumped into my head, and I still have no idea what it means. Every now and then, especially lately, a disconnected sentence or some foggy image comes to me when least expected. I puzzle over it, try to pull some meaning from it, and get nowhere. Like now.

I'll let you feed the rabbits . . . if.

If what? And what *about* rabbits?

"Adri? He's here! Ryan's here." The bedroom door opens and Mom sticks her head in.

"Be right there."

Mom's face appears in the mirror beside mine, watchful, anxious. I want to say, "Please don't worry. It's all right. Really, Mom." But it would do no good.

7

"He's such a nice young man," she says. "Isn't he?"

"Very." I give her a reassuring smile and for a moment let myself visualize Ryan's face. Angular, with widespread, thoughtful eyes. Kind eyes. A head of red-brown hair usually in need of cutting. The girls say he has a sensuous mouth and ask if he's a good lover.

I shiver and reach for my shawl.

Mom settles on the edge of my bed as I drape the shawl around my shoulders. "You've known him—what is it— two months now?" she asks.

"About." I stuff some money, a comb, the house keys into my purse, snap it shut, and stand up. *Not now, Mom, please. Not again!*

"That's longer than with anyone else."

"I guess."

"He must really like you to ask you to his family's Christmas party."

"Oh, Mom!" I start to the door.

"Well, it's true. Before Ryan you'd have one, two, maybe three dates with a boy and you were through with him. So Ryan must be very special."

I glance back at her, wondering if she really believes what she says or is she just trying to be diplomatic? It isn't that *I'm* through with a boy. What always happens is that after three or four dates when I won't . . . can't . . . Well, after a while, *he* doesn't ask *me* out again.

"Ryan's waiting," I say at the doorway.

"Yes." Mom gets up and follows me. In the hall she whispers, "I'm sorry, honey. I know I hassle you too much about some things, but all I want is for you to be happy."

In the moment before we enter the living room, our eyes meet and we exchange the same confused signals we've been exchanging for as long as I can remember. When she starts probing, I close up inside, as tight as a nut. I can actually feel myself going blank. At the same time *she* gets a hopeful expression in her eyes, which very quickly turns to hurt. "Some girls tell their mothers nearly everything," she once told me. And I had no answer.

It's probably my fault, and I'm sorry. But that's the way I am. I just can't talk about a lot of things Mom would like me to share.

Ryan jumps up from the couch and his face brightens as soon as I come into the room. A little pulse of excitement hits me, too. He'd come to me, but Becky, my little sister, holds him back, pulling at his sweater. He puts a hand on her head and says, "Down, clown."

I laugh. Becky is at it with him, too. She just started preschool and is driving us batty rhyming. Mom says to be patient, that I went through that same stage when I was in nursery school. The same school as Becky goes to, in fact. Which shows they haven't changed their curriculum much in twelve years.

"Ryan lion!" Becky cries triumphantly, dancing around Ryan. "Wabbit gwabbit!"

"Rabbit," Mom corrects. "And it's your bedtime, Miss Rhyme Princess. So say good-night to Adri and Ryan and come along with me."

"Give Adri a big hug first," I say, hunching down to little person's height and opening my arms. Becky flies into them and I lift her high, bringing her soft, smooth cheek close to my own, smelling her little-girl sweetness and laughing with pleasure.

When I set her down she runs back to Ryan, hugging him around the legs as if she'll never let go. Ryan seems pleased, but a little uneasy too.

This time Mom won't let Becky get her way with postponing bedtime. In her best schoolteacher voice she says, "Come along, ducky lucky. Time for one story, then beddy-bye." She pries Becky loose, and my sister goes along like a little lamb, thumb plugged securely in her mouth. "Have fun tonight, you two. See you in the morning, Adri," Mom calls, looking back once.

And then I am alone with Ryan.

I guess I am shy. Mom says that's my trouble. She's given me umpteen articles and books on how to make conversation and feel confident in groups or one-on-one. I read all the stuff and even try to put some of the ideas to work. But no matter what, those first minutes with a date, no matter how well we got on the last time together, are just awful for me. All the light seems to leave the room. I drop things, bump into people. My mind stops working. I don't even hear what the other person is saying, I'm so into myself.

For too long I stand facing Ryan with this stiff little smile on my face. Ryan raises an eyebrow and says, "So

. . . let's go," and we both giggle, thinking of Becky. Then he takes my arm and we head for the door.

"Your sister's quite a charmer," he says as we go down the driveway to his car. "Precocious, too."

"Sure is," I agreed. "She's starting to read already."

"Mmm," he says, after a little pause. "That's not quite what I mean. But you're right. She sure is grown up for a three-and-a-half-year-old."

With that we climb into his car and drive the short distance to his house, where the family Christmas party is in progress.

I can see the holiday atmosphere from the street. The two-story, white brick home is decorated with Christmas lights, and a festive wreath is hung on the front door. Through the picture windows I see people moving about and glimpse a snow-tipped tree, its bright ornaments and tinsel adding to the feeling of warmth.

I must seem anxious, because Ryan puts a warm hand on my icy one as he turns off the ignition. "They're all family and friends. Nothing to worry about," he says. "I do have to put in an appearance, and Mom says she'd like to meet you. And besides, the food is fan-tastic." He watches me, then adds, "We don't have to stay all evening."

"I'm sorry." I turn toward him. "It's just that I hate crowds. It makes me feel so uncomfortable. I feel as if everyone's watching me, and I just freeze. Mom says it's terribly egotistical to feel like that, that the whole world isn't hanging on my next word." I shrug. "She's right, I know, but it doesn't change the way I feel."

"We all feel self-conscious when we're thrown in with a bunch of strangers," Ryan says. "Even me."

"Not you."

"Believe it, Adri. Behind that confident, boyish grin and friendly manner there's a sweaty brow, clammy hands, and wobbly knees."

I have to think about that for a moment, because I've always seen Ryan as self-confident and poised, way beyond his age. "Even so," I say. "Please, Ryan. Don't leave me alone."

"Promise," he says. "Now, let's go slay the dragon." He jumps out of the car and runs around to open the door for me. Hand in hand we amble up the brick walk to the front door.

Greeting the guests are Ryan's parents—his mother pretty, slender, and bubbly; his father tall, sturdy, and with the same dark, intelligent eyes as Ryan's.

Mrs. O'Connor gives me a hug. "I'm so glad you could come. Ryan says such nice things about you."

Mr. O'Connor winks at Ryan. "I see you have as good taste in women as your father." Before we can reply, new visitors arrive and Ryan's parents turn to greet them.

"What did you tell your mother about me?" I whisper as Ryan hangs my shawl in a hall closet.

"That you're just my type. A little wild. Crazy about me. And very sexy." He glances at me sideways.

I know he's joking, but there's so much unspoken behind those teasing words that I get warm all over.

12

"You are, aren't you?" Ryan gives me this penetrating stare.

"Absolutely." I keep my voice light, but look away and tremble.

"Adrienne?"

I swing around, still burning from Ryan's challenge. In a group of new arrivals, waiting to deposit their wraps, stands a tall, slender woman in a green wool coat with fur collar. Her short, white hair, cut like a man's, frames a face with thin lips and blue eyes. I step back, bumping into Ryan.

"Adrienne Meyer. It is, isn't it? I never forget a face."

My heart starts pounding and my mouth goes dry. Other guests smile, hang their coats, watch with interest. Ryan's hands on my shoulders should be reassuring but they're not. I hate myself for this terrible shyness; it's like a disease.

"Oh, my dear. You really don't remember, do you? Martha Plunkett? You know. The Treehouse Preschool? I've seen you when you come to pick up Becky sometimes. What is it? Twelve, thirteen years since you were a student? You were such a wonderful, bright little thing."

Yes, yes. Now I know. But she's changed. Thinner. Wrinkles around the cheeks. Lines under the eyes. Yet they are the same eyes, watery blue and commanding. In a blue polyester dress, with pearls over the nearly flat bosom, she is the original "sweet little old lady from Pasadena."

"Oh, yes! Ms. Plunkett," I say as she holds out a hand.

13

My own is moist and cold and I keep it to myself. "This is Ryan O'Connor, my friend," I say.

"So you're the O'Connor boy I've heard so much about! I know your mother well. We serve together on several child welfare committees. Lovely woman, your mother." Plunkett smiles radiantly at us as a young couple approaches. The woman exclaims, "Martha!" and puts an arm around Ms. Plunkett. "How very nice to see you!"

The three start talking about a fund-raiser for the preschool. Ryan whispers, "Bor-ing!" and we make our escape. As soon as I turn my back, Plunkett calls out, "Remember me to your parents, Adrienne!"

Ryan introduces me to lots of relatives and family friends, and then we go into the dining room to fill our plates from a table laden with marvelous foods. Everything smells and looks so good—platters of ham and beef, hot casseroles, salads, and wonderful sweets. People nearby joke with us and everyone complains about putting on too much weight.

We take our plates to a side room to eat and talk about leaving soon, when the music starts. Someone is at the piano in the living room, playing Christmas carols. People start moving toward the sound.

"On the first day of Christmas . . ."

"Let's . . ." I put my plate down on a table and hold a hand out to Ryan. I sing softly, "My true love gave to me . . ." Ryan sings the next line with me as we walk into the living room.

Ryan's mother is playing, a look on her face of peace, love, and joy. Behind her stands Mr. O'Connor, one hand on her shoulder, his deep voice booming out the lyrics. Guests, some with drinks in hand, or with arms around loved ones, join in. I lean my head back against Ryan and close my eyes. It feels so good to sing, to be here. I feel so much trust and hope, goodness and love here in this group that I almost cry.

When I open my eyes I see, directly across the piano from us, Martha Plunkett. She is watching me, a thoughtful, almost guarded look on her face. When our eyes meet, she smiles, but my heart begins to pound again.

For no reason that I can possibly understand I hear again in my head, *I'll let you feed the rabbits . . . if . . .*

Chapter 2

"Where to now, Adrienne Hadrian?"

I laugh. The night air is clear and crisp, typical of California in late December. The moon is full and the mountains are silhouetted against the sky.

Ryan shadowboxes around me as we leave the house. He's so full of energy, he's like a puppy let off the leash, and there's a special sparkle to his eyes.

I know what he wants me to say—and I can't say it.

"Let's just drive around and see the Christmas decorations," I say brightly. "Then we can go to Bev's house. She's having a few of the guys over."

Some of the sparkle fades and he stops shadowboxing. I know he's disappointed. He'd rather we'd drive to the Lookout. The valley view should be fantastic tonight, though that's not what kids drive up there for. "If that's what you want." He opens the car door for me, but he sounds hurt.

"We've plenty of time." I put a hand on Ryan's arm for an instant, pleading patience and understanding. "I don't have to be home until one."

"Right." There's a sharpness to his voice now. "So long as we make some time just for us."

"Of course!" In the darkness it's easy to sound positive. After all, the evening has just begun. But what of later, when I can't postpone anymore?

We drive to Christmas Tree Lane first. It's traditional to walk along the two-block street each Christmas season, because the houses and trees are so beautifully decorated. Deodar trees, not palms, line the streets, and fake snow covers the lawns of some homes so you can almost forget you're in California.

"I remember Christmas when I was a kid," Ryan says as we walk hand in hand along the street. "It wasn't phony, like this."

"I guess you need snow and cold for Christmas to be real," I say.

Ryan nods. "The day before Christmas we'd drive out of the city early in the day to go to my grandparents, upstate. I can still hear the swish-swish of the wipers clearing away the snow from the windshield. I can still smell my wet mittens and cap." Ryan chuckles quietly and I smile to myself.

"I'd press my nose against the cold window and try to take in everything: people rushing along the wind-driven streets . . . kids on sleds . . . ice-skaters on frozen ponds . . . and outside the city the little towns covered with clean blankets of snow."

Carolers approach and stand under a streetlamp. We stop talking to listen as their voices fill the mild California night. And then we move on.

17

"When we got to my grandparents, the whole family would be there," Ryan continues. "Aunts, uncles, cousins—lots of cousins. Boy, was there noise! Laughter and talk and babies crying—and food!"

"Sounds nice," I say longingly.

Ryan turns to me in surprise. "Wasn't your holiday anything like that?"

I try to remember Christmases past, but it's as if life didn't start until I was six or seven. Everything before that is lost. So I tell him what I do recall.

"We don't have family out here. My parents came to California right after they were married. They left sisters and brothers and parents in the East. So when there were special events, like birthdays, or Thanksgiving, or Christmas—we had no one except each other. Maybe we'd go to dinner and a movie—or have a feast at home. Until recently. We have some friends—the Golds." I smile at the thought. "They always make parties on the Fourth of July and Christmas. They don't have kids, so they invite all their friends with children—friends who are like us, without roots—and they've made kind of a family of friends. I meet the same kids there each year, and we're sort of like cousins. It's nice."

We walk back to his car two blocks away, talking of other special childhood memories. Ryan recalls the first time he flew a kite: the kite got away. He was only four, and he cried. I nod in the darkness, understanding how he must have felt.

"I remember pretty far back. Do you?" he asks.

Again I search my mind for early memories and find

none. I can't even picture myself at Becky's age. It's as if a whole chunk of time has been wiped out.

"What were you like?" he asks, almost reading my thoughts.

"I don't know. I've seen pictures, but it's as if they're of someone else. I wish I *could* remember," I say wistfully. "Maybe life was so uneventful then that it wasn't worth remembering."

"Maybe," Ryan says. "And maybe it'll all come back some time."

And then we're at Bev's house.

Beverly Crowder has been my best friend since sixth grade, when we discovered Judy Blume books together. From then on we devoured everything Blume ever wrote, even the books we weren't supposed to read because they had so much "sex" in them. And then we'd giggle about them and talk about them for hours. We couldn't believe our own parents did such weird things as the books described. We couldn't imagine ourselves ever doing such things. For that matter, we could never even imagine any boy liking us enough to ask us out, much less want to make love to us.

But that was years ago. Now Bev and I still talk, but about lots of other things—the world, God, life, our families. And sex too. In fact, it seems to me that sex is the subject Bev likes most these days. Ever since she started dating Jason.

"They're in Bev's room, playing Trivial Pursuit," Mrs. Crowder says when she answers the door. "Go on in, honey, and tell her the oatmeal cookies are ready."

"I'll bring them," I say. The house smells of cinnamon and oatmeal as we follow Mrs. Crowder into the warm kitchen. Bev's sister Sunny, home from college until after the new year, is at a table shelling walnuts. She greets me, but her eyes are on Ryan, and as Bev's mom and I arrange the cookies on a platter, she talks to him about college.

Bev says that ever since Sunny got home the house has been a zoo. Phone calls. Kids dropping by. Arguments. "And she's hardly ever around. She sleeps until noon and goes to bed long after everyone else. My dad says he doesn't see why he paid for her ticket to come home since he never gets to see her."

I don't know about the arguments, because right now Sunny seems to have the sweetest, sunniest personality of anyone I ever met. When we finally leave the kitchen, she says, "See you around, Ryan." At the last moment she adds, "And Adri."

We go into Bev's room, where she's playing Trivial Pursuit with Jason, Marissa, and Dan. They're sitting cross-legged on the floor with the game board spread out between them, cola cans and chips nearby.

"Ta-*dah!*" Ryan announces. He steps aside as I come in like a head waiter, cookie tray raised high.

"Beware of friends bearing oatmeal cookies," I say in an ominous tone. Bev's round face blooms into a warm smile. She jumps up to take the tray from me, and they all move over to include us on the floor.

These are my real friends. I feel comfortable with them. It's not just that we always find lots to talk about together; it's that we don't make judgments and don't put each other down like a lot of kids I could name.

The Trivial Pursuit game is well under way. Dan Sato is winning, with Marissa next, Jason, and then Bev. I don't really see how Bev could be doing so badly, because when we play, she's very good.

"It's my turn," Bev says, taking the die. She rolls and checks the board for where to land. She has a choice of history or entertainment and chooses the latter.

Jason picks out a question card and reads, "What actress played the role of Little Miss Marker in 1934?"

Bev knows the answer. I'm sure of it because just this week we were talking about Shirley Temple Black and the time she was a U.S. representative to the United Nations.

But she looks puzzled, wrinkling up her forehead and gazing coyly at Jason. "Gee . . . I don't know. Judy Garland?"

"Oh, poor muppet," Jason says, giving her an affectionate hug. "Garland was in the forties, . . . not the thirties. It's Shirley Temple."

I'm about to say something when she gives me a little warning nod. "What difference does it make?" she's asking me. And I wonder, how can she act like an airhead just so Jason can feel superior?

The game breaks up soon after, and everyone gets up to stretch. And then Jason puts on the stereo so we can dance.

A couple of numbers are fast, but then there are three pieces in a row that are real slow and romantic. Jason

21

flips off the lamps and closes the door so that only a crack of light shows. Dan and Marissa are giggling in the dark on the bed. Jason and Bev are dancing so close you couldn't put a sheet of paper between them.

Ryan holds his arms out to me.

"It's dark in here," I whisper as we dance together.

"Good." He presses me close, both hands around my back.

"Kind of crowded," I say, bumping into Bev. I giggle. "You tickle. You need a shave."

"Mmmm," Ryan grunts.

"I wonder how you'd look with a beard." Ryan doesn't answer, and I know he wishes I'd shut up, but I can't. Words tumble out of my mouth. Sometimes, when I'm with a boy who tries to get romantic, I make remarks about everything around me to get his mind off sex.

Ryan's eyes are closed. He wants to enjoy the music and me. But my eyes are open, wide open, and I'm watching everyone. Bev and Jason are glued together in a long kiss. Marissa is sitting on Dan's lap.

It's terribly hot in the room. I whisper, "Ryan. Let's go."

He doesn't respond at first and his breathing isn't normal, but then he says, "Why?"

"I don't feel . . ." I stop myself from saying *comfortable* and say instead, "I'm due home in an hour."

"Oh . . . oh . . . yes." He releases me very reluctantly and takes my hand instead. I get my wrap from the bed and we slip away with murmured good-byes.

"I have something to show you," Ryan says when we

22

settle in his car after leaving Bev's house. It's almost midnight and I feel myself growing more anxious with each minute. There's no more postponing. Ryan is going to want to go where we can be alone together.

He stretches behind the front seat and retrieves a plastic sack which seems at first to be empty. He digs inside it and pulls out a package. "Here," he says triumphantly. "A little Christmas present."

I have so many different feelings all at the same time—surprise, delight, curiosity, awe—as he holds the package out to me. "But—but Ryan!" I protest. "I didn't get *you* anything."

"Doesn't matter. I don't care. Go ahead. Open it."

It's the first time in my life that a boy has ever given me a present. I wonder if it's right to take it. Does it mean anything? What will Mom say? And then I think suddenly that accepting this gift brings with it a kind of debt.

"I . . . I don't think . . ."

"Adri, Adri. It's no big thing, honestly. Go on, see what I bought."

Reluctantly I take the package, hefting it and making outrageous guesses about its contents even though it feels like it has to be a book. Attached to the gold ribbon is a small card which reads simply, "For Adri. Ryan." I look up at Ryan and smile, then undo the wrapping.

It's a beautiful leather-bound book in a deep wine color with gold-leaf designs that make it seem Italian. Inside are lined pages.

"Oh, Ryan," I exclaim as tears rush to my eyes. "It's lovely." I run my fingers over the butter-soft leather.

Ryan bends close. "Look. See? It's just right for the poetry you like to write. You can use it as a diary, if you want. Or to write stories in. Or for anything."

"It's so . . . fine . . ."

"Like you, Adri."

"No. Not like me."

"Oh, yes." He runs a finger down my cheek, and his eyes get a cloudy look. He leans close and kisses me. Once tentatively, then once again. Then he backs off to see my reaction.

My hands are clutching the book against me like a shield. I so want to feel what I know is in my heart for Ryan, but I can sense my body stiffening, just as always.

"Adri . . ." he whispers.

"I . . . I want to, Ryan. It's okay . . ."

But of course it isn't. As he holds me close, the heat of his face against mine makes me want to scream. I can't breathe. I feel nauseous. If I don't stop I may be sick.

"Ryan . . ." I have to speak his name a second time before he comes back from where he was.

"Ryan. It's late. I promised to be home by one."

The digital clock on the dashboard flashes 12:29. Ryan sees it, says nothing, pulls back, and sits stiffly against his seat, staring out the window.

"Don't you like me at all, Adri?" he asks finally.

"Yes . . . yes . . . a lot."

"Then why? Do you find me repulsive or something?"

"No . . . no. Not that."

"We've been going together almost three months now. You don't even like me to kiss you."

24

My throat feels like I just swallowed dry toast. "I'm sorry." I whisper.

"Is that all you can say?"

"Yes!! I don't know why I'm this way, but if it matters that much, find someone else to go with. Why bother with me?"

He takes my hands but I can't bring myself to look at him. "When we first started going out I realized you weren't easy to know. But I figured it would be worth waiting because in the end I'd find a whole lot more with you than with most of the other girls I've met."

"You're wrong."

"I don't think so."

I want to ask if all this means he'll stop seeing me. I want to tell him that I really can't help myself, that I don't want to be like this. I want to say, "Please, give me more time." But I can't. Pride gets in the way.

In the semidarkness I see Ryan shrug. He drops my hands and turns back to the wheel. He starts the ignition and pulls out of the parking space.

"Where are we going?"

"Home." He has nothing more to say for the rest of the drive. When he pulls into our driveway I open my door as soon as he cuts the engine.

"Wait!" Ryan grabs my hand and holds me there.

"What!"

"Take the book."

"I don't want it." What I mean is—the book has strings attached.

"Take it, Adri. I want you to have it."

I take the book and start to get out of the car again. "Adri?"

In the moonlight I see Ryan clearly. He's resigned—an expression I've seen before—and hurt and puzzled too. I want to touch his face but fear he'll misunderstand.

"Listen," he says. "I won't press you. The way I feel about you I have only two choices. Quit seeing you altogether . . . or be patient."

There's a long silence before I say, "I can't promise anything."

He laughs suddenly. "If the guys only knew the truth . . . I'd be the laughingstock of the school."

"If the girls ever knew, they'd think I was crazy."

"I won't tell," he says, "if you don't."

For a long moment we gaze fondly at each other. Then I lean into the car and give Ryan a quick kiss. "Thanks," I whisper, and then turn and run down the walk to the house.

Chapter 3

The first day of school after the new year we all wake late. During the night a Santa Ana condition began. The desert winds blew loud and wild, making it hard to sleep. Not only that, but the power went out, so our alarm clocks didn't wake us.

So it's frantic time. It's after eight, and Mom was due at her school more than a half hour ago. Dad's upstairs dressing. I'm in the kitchen making Becky's lunch. Mom is standing in the hallway trying to get Becky into a sweater. Her hair is kind of wild, and she hasn't taken time to put on makeup.

"Mark!" she calls upstairs. "I'm late! Can you drop Becky at school?" She calls in to me, "Is her lunch ready?"

"Almost!" I bag the egg salad sandwich and reach for an apple.

"Can't!" Dad shouts down. "I was due in court ten minutes ago!"

"Shoot!" Mom mumbles. "Becky, stop squirming! Come on, in for breakfast. Shoot! What am I going to do?"

This is an important day for Mom. Some big shots from the county are coming to evaluate the school. The principal expects all the teachers to be at their best.

I come out of the kitchen with Becky's Miss Piggy lunchbox. "Here, I put a banana inside and a can of orange juice. She can eat breakfast while you drive."

"Adri . . . can you?" Mom opens her purse and runs a lipstick quickly over her lips without checking the mirror. "If it was any other day . . . !"

"I'll take her. I have free first period today, so it really doesn't matter. . . . Go on."

"No, no!" Becky cries, grabbing hold of Mom's skirt. "I want Mommy! Mommy!"

For an instant Mom looks distraught. As usual she's torn between family and job. But even so she's already getting into her coat and picking up the briefcase full of books and papers.

"Becky, stop it!" I say. "Go on, Mom. She'll be okay." I pull Becky off Mom, which sets her to screaming even louder.

Mom gives my sister a quick kiss on the head, but I can see how hard it is for her to leave, so I give her a push and repeat not to worry. We'll be fine.

The door opens. Mom disappears, and I'm left with a screaming three-year-old.

"Okay, Becky-wecky, *enough!* Didn't you tell me you're going to have a special surprise today at school, hmm?" I draw my sister into the kitchen and sit her down on a chair. She's crying softly now, thumb in mouth, but her attention is fully on me.

"What kind of surprise do you think it will be?" I ask, pouring Cheerios into a bowl and adding milk. I bring the banana to the table from the lunchbox and offer to peel it for Becky.

Becky is keyed to the school surprise now, already forgetting Mom has left. Her big brown eyes, glistening with tears, brighten with thought. I spoon some of the cereal into her mouth, all the time talking quietly about the wonderful surprise in store for her. Will they go on a trip to the zoo? Will she get the chance to play in the rocket ship today? Is today the day she'll get to feed the goldfish? At the same time I'm watching the clock and wondering if I'll be able to get to second period on time, considering the preschool is four miles from home and seven from the high school.

Dad comes into the room, distractedly pours himself some coffee, grimaces as he burns his mouth, looks out the window at the magnolia he planted last spring—it's bent almost to the ground—and shakes his head impatiently. "Be good, you two." He puts down the cup and grabs his attaché case. "See you tonight. Adri? You can manage?"

"Sure," I say. "Don't worry."

It's good to see Dad's relieved but brief smile, and I think how hard it must be for Mom and him to balance everything—jobs, the house, time for our problems, time for theirs and each other. I don't think I ever want to get married. It's too hard.

With one eye on my watch, I manage to down some breakfast, get Becky toileted, and run up to my room to get my books. Becky follows and immediately goes for the book Ryan bought me, on my desk. So far, I have copied only one poem into it, written during the holidays.

"Pretty," Becky says, picking it up before I can stop her.

"Give that to me!" I bellow. "You'll get your dirty fingers all over it! And don't ever touch it again, you hear?" I'm sorry immediately for sounding so mean, but Becky has it coming. She has no respect for my things. Last week she found my stapler and stapled every sheet of paper on my desk. A few weeks ago she emptied my bottom dresser drawer to make a bed for her dolls.

Frightened at my tone, she backs off, and I put the book high up on a shelf where she won't be able to reach.

Luckily we catch a bus almost immediately, and soon we're on the street leading to the preschool. The wind is gusting again, pushing against us with frightening force. It moans and howls and yanks cruelly at the leaves and branches, tearing them from the trees and chasing them past us in great clumps. A particularly severe gust takes my breath away and I stop in the middle of the street to gather Becky close.

My heart begins to pound, but not from the wind. There is a memory, as wispy as fog, trying to take shape, and I want not to see it. It's of another time. There is wind, like today. Something about how these leaves fly, this way and that, as if pursued, reminds me of . . . of . . . helplessness and terror. I bury my face in Becky's

30

hair and hear myself whimper. And then the wind sub-
sides. And I can breathe again.

"Were you scared too, Adri?" Becky asks as we con-
tinue down the street to the corner.

"Yes, Becky. But it was just the wind, and it's okay
now."

The Treehouse Preschool is on the corner of a pleas-
ant street in a residential neighborhood. It's a one-story
building, formerly a private home, surrounded by a
picket fence. The school's name is very tastefully dis-
played in Gothic gold leaf on a small white board.

A magnificent California oak dominates the front yard,
which is strewn today with debris from the wind. Nailed
to the trunk is a wood ladder that leads to a large branch
on which is a treehouse, a replica of the preschool. This
isn't the same location I went to as a child. Three years
ago Plunkett bought this larger house so she could handle twice the number of children as in my time.

Because of the wind, parents aren't just dropping their
children off at the corner today and watching while the
kids go to the front gate where a teacher waits. Instead,
they park and walk their children to the gate.

It's a while since I've seen so many kids, Becky's age
and younger, together. They seem so little and innocent
and vulnerable. I put an arm around my sister's thin
shoulder as we approach the gate and whisper that I'm
sorry I yelled at her. She responds with "I love you,
Adwi."

"Love you too, Becky-wecky."

And then Mrs. T arrives. She's a pleasant-faced,

grandmotherly-looking woman who introduces herself to me and greets Becky with a happy "Good morning, dear. Isn't the wind exciting?" She knows each child by name and has a way of engaging each immediately with an appropriate question. "Did Santa come to your house, Danny?" "Hello, Charlene. How are the new puppies?"

Becky launches into a long story about the wind. She asks what happens to birds when it blows so hard—and asks if they will fly kites today. She has already made the transition from me to the teacher.

Mrs. T, like a Pied Piper, speaks wordlessly to the mothers as she separates them from their children. Then, singing "It's off to school we go," she guides them down the path into the schoolhouse.

I look after them, hoping Becky will turn and wave good-bye, but her trusting face is lifted toward Mrs. T. I am already forgotten.

As I turn away, keyed once more to the late hour and the fact that the bus is due at the corner in three minutes, a car stops at the curb. A young mother in tennis skirt and sweater jumps out and runs around to open the door on the passenger side. She lifts a small boy out of the seat. He is screaming and fighting, holding on to the steering wheel with all his might.

"Now, Greg, just stop that!" his mother cries, tugging at him. "It's going to be fun. You know you love Ms. Plunkett. Stop it!" By the set of her lips I can see that she's at the end of her patience, and as we pass, the child is not only screaming but kicking at her. She smacks him hard. "Now, that's enough!" Catching my eye she says, "You know how it is—especially with boys . . . and especially after a holiday." She gives me a weak smile and holds her son more gently.

Cheerful Mrs. T is back, hands extended in welcome. "Come along, Greg. You don't want Mommy to think you're a baby. We have a wonderful surprise for you today. Remember? Come on, dear." She pries the clinging child from his mother, saying "He'll be happy as a lark in five minutes, so don't you worry one bit." Then, while he continues to kick and scream, she carries him down the path into the house.

A lump forms in my chest. He's such a baby. Must he be civilized so young just so his mother can go play tennis? I don't care what Mom and Dad say about preschool being good for children, helping prepare them for regular school.

And then I deliberately close my heart to it all because it's late and I've taken much too much time already. I have to run or miss the bus.

Bev and I haven't talked since the New Year's party at Jason's home two days ago, so there's lots to go over. When we catch up with each other outside the economics classroom, Bev is waiting. She looks like she's bursting to tell me something.

"We've got to talk."

"Sure, when?" Kids are streaming into the room, bumping us. She'll be late for her next class unless she hurries. "After school?"

She shakes her head. "I'm going to watch Jason practice."

The bell rings. "Tonight? I could come over."

"Super!" She turns and runs down the hall, calling back, "Around eight!"

And so, that evening, I go to Bev's right after supper.

She answers the door and holds a finger to her lips as we pass the living room. It seems her parents are having an argument with Sunny, something about when she leaves to return to college.

"She wants to stay with her boyfriend for a couple days," Bev whispers as we pass.

"What's wrong with that?"

"Not at his parents' home—get it?"

"Oh."

When we reach her room, Bev locks the door behind us and pounces on the bed.

I look around for where to sit. The bed, the chairs, everything is full of clothes. Neatness is not one of Bev's strong points.

"Sit anywhere." She gets up and starts gathering up jeans and sweaters, balling them into a big bundle. She stands in the middle of the room wearing a puzzled expression and says, "Darn. It's too much trouble to put away." With a devilish grin, she leans over her mattress and drops the bundle on the floor between bed and wall. Then she plants herself on the mattress lotus fashion, and pats a spot opposite for me to sit. Still whispering, she says, "She was *dumb*. She let Mom hear her on the phone. She's always telling me that Mom and Dad don't

34

have to know everything, that what they don't know won't hurt them. And here she is on the phone with her boyfriend, where she knows Mom can hear. *Dumb!*"

"Does she love him?"

"I don't know. Does it matter?"

"Hey, Bev. Sure it does."

"Maybe it doesn't. Maybe she just wants to experiment a little, find out what it's like with different guys."

I feel out of my depth. Until Jason, Bev would never talk this way. "How did it go at the New Year's party, after we left?" I ask, changing the subject.

I am referring to the party I went to with Ryan at Jason's house. Jase's parents were away, skiing in Aspen, so he had the house to himself. We all brought something. I made an onion dip and Ryan brought a six-pack of cola. There were probably twenty of us; so there was lots to eat and drink.

The evening started slowly, with lots of talk and jokes and dancing. By midnight we were all pretty high from the excitement of New Year's and knowing we were unchaperoned. Some of the kids were drinking, and not just Cokes, so several in the group were pretty loud—or slowed down, depending on how the booze affected them.

Just before midnight Jason turned on the radio and we all counted down with the announcer, and then Jason turned out the lights and everyone kissed. Ryan kissed me tenderly and held me close a long time until one of the other guys poked him and said, "My turn."

Little by little I found myself getting more tense. I just

don't like guys I hardly know grabbing and kissing me. Someone even put his tongue in my mouth. After that I ran into the bathroom and nearly puked.

When I came back into the playroom, the lights were on again and everyone was blowing horns and clacking clackers and shouting "Happy New Year!" And then Jason got up on a table and said, "Hey guys! I have a great idea."

Ryan slipped over to stand beside me and put an arm through mine.

"Let's go skinny-dipping!"

"Yeah! Great idea!"

"Hey, let's go!"

"Where do we change?"

Laughter. "You mean, where do we undress?"

I must have gotten as stiff as a board, because Ryan whispered, "You don't have to, Adri."

Without answering, I started to edge away. I didn't even want his hand on me.

"Hey, where are you going, Adri?" Jason called. "The fun's just starting."

"They want to be a . . . *lone,*" one of the boys called out. He whistled, making a lot of the kids laugh.

"Let's get out of here," Ryan said in the hall. "Come on, Adri. I'll get your coat."

And so Ryan and I spent the rest of New Year's Eve just driving around. We talked about everything except why I got so upset. He told me that probably other kids didn't want to go skinny-dipping either, and wouldn't. He told me that Bev had looked very embarrassed, "kind of stunned, so don't feel you were the only one."

"Did *you* go skinny-dipping," I ask Bev.

Her face turns scarlet and she starts plucking at the little loops on her blue bedspread. Bev's very self-conscious about her body because she's on the plump side. She's always on a diet, but whenever things go wrong—a poor test grade, no call from Jason—she binges. I can't imagine she'd be able to undress down to her birthday suit. "Did you go skinny-dipping?" I repeat.

"Sort of," she says.

"What's sort of?"

"I kept my bra and panties on." She looks up, and a tear glistens in her eye. "But you should have seen them. Most of the girls stripped, and all the guys." She looks away. "I never saw a guy in the nude before." She pauses. "They laughed at me because I wouldn't take everything off."

I don't answer.

"Jason said . . ." She stops. "Jason said . . . I'm better endowed . . . that's why I didn't . . ." She giggles with embarrassment. "It was dark, so you couldn't see all that much. . . . Actually, it was pretty exciting."

I am watching her and don't know how I feel. Would it have been so awful to do what she did—go with the others but keep my underclothes on? "Did anyone say anything about our leaving early?"

"We all assumed you were going off somewhere to make out. Did you?"

I hesitate, then say, "Sure."

"You know, Adri," Bev says, putting a hand on my arm. "We always told each other everything. Lately I get the feeling that you're holding back. I tell you everything —you know exactly how far I've gone with Jason. How about you?"

This is the time for me to tell my best friend how it is, how I feel about being close. How I feel about being hugged, even by my mother. I wrap my arms around myself and look down.

"Well?" Bev asks.

I feel very sad as I meet Bev's eyes. "There's nothing to tell."

"You're kidding. What's the matter? He isn't gay, is he?"

I laugh. "No."

"Then what?"

I shake my head and close my eyes and rock back and forth, closing myself into a cocoon that is far away from where I am.

And that strange phrase comes into my head again.

I'll let you feed the rabbits . . . if . . .

Chapter 4

"It's a wabbit, Adwi! A wabbit! My vewy own wabbit!" Becky squeals, hurling herself at me as soon as she comes into the kitchen with Mom, from school.

Mom lays a bag of groceries on the counter and shakes her head. "R-r-r-rabbit, sweetheart. Say it: R-r-rabbit!" To me she adds, "She's been this way from the minute I picked her up after school. I've never seen her so excited."

"Was that the surprise, sweetie?" I hunch down to eye level with my sister. "Was that it?"

"Yes, yes, yes, yes! Ms. Plunkett gave me my vewy own wabb—bunny!" She glances quickly at Mom and then back to me. "It's a *she*. She's so soft and white, like snow, and she has this little pink nose and I got to hold her and name her and . . ."

"What did you name her?"

"Noel said to call her Fuzzy, and Jonathan said Whitey, but I thought and thought and I named her Petah!"

"Peter? But that's a boy's name, Becky."

It stops her for just an instant, and then she says, "I don't care. Her name is Petah Wabbit."

39

"Rabbit," Mom says.

"Wabbit."

While I help Mom put groceries away, Becky climbs up on the stool at the breakfast bar and chatters on happily about school and the rabbit and how she'll get to care for it. I am putting lettuce and a clump of broccoli in the vegetable bin of the fridge and only half listening when something Becky says turns me cold. I straighten up and turn around.

"What? What did you say, Becky?"

"Adri, shut the refrigerator door," Mom calls out.

"Becky. What did you just say?" I slam the door and lean across the breakfast bar so my face is close to Becky's.

"What's with you, Adrienne?" Mom asks. "All she's been talking about is that rabbit and how they're going to let her feed him, her, whatever—carrots and stuff. Now help me get the rest of this food put away."

"Becky. Say it again, please, just the way you did before."

By this time Mom has stopped what she's doing and has come to stand beside me. She puts a hand on my arm and asks, "Adri . . . what's wrong?"

Becky must have heard something different in my voice, too, because her eyes open wide in alarm. She looks from me to Mom as if maybe she said something wrong. She may even cry.

"It's okay, honey. Just tell me what it is you said about Ms. Plunkett."

"Ms. Plunkett," Becky begins slowly, still looking to Mom for reassurance, "she said, 'I'll let you feed the wabbit . . .'"

I gasp.

And then Becky adds, "'If you're a good girl.'"

"Oh!" I take a deep, deep breath and back away. "Is *that* it!" Suddenly I feel wonderful and start to laugh.

"What's going on? Adri, are you all right?" Mom asks.

I wipe the tears of relief from my face and smile back at her. "Oh, yes! Everything's just fine, Mom! Really. Isn't it just wonderful that Becky's got a rabbit?"

"How was the New Year's party?" Mom asks as we fix dinner together that evening. While I wash the salad greens to put in the spinner, Mom grates cheddar cheese for the beef enchilada casserole.

It seems so long ago already that I say, "The party? Oh. It was fine."

"Is that all you can say? Honestly, Adrienne, you're as closed as a sphinx. Surely there's something you can share with *me*, your mother." Her peevish glance glides over me as she throws a handful of grated cheese into a bowl. "You might tell me who was there, what you did . . . if you had fun. For heaven's sake, you act as if I'm some kind of ogre. Am I so terrible? Do I criticize? Do I judge you?"

"I'm sorry, Mom, it's just that there isn't really much to say. It was a party. There were maybe twenty kids. At Jason's house."

41

"Were his parents there?"

"No."

A brief pressing together of lips shows the disapproval, but her voice remains steady. "Was it fun?"

"Yes. We danced and talked—you know, the usual things you do at a party."

"How late did it last?"

"I don't know. We left just after midnight. Everyone was going swimming in their pool, and I—we decided to leave."

"I see." She pauses, and I know what she's thinking. *She left the party around midnight, but didn't get home until two hours later.* "And then what?"

Is there hope in her voice? Is she asking if we spent the next two hours making out? Will that make her feel there's nothing wrong with me after all?

"We drove around and talked. We stopped in at an all-night coffee shop and had some hot chocolate, and then we came home."

The lips press together again. Silently she dips the tortillas into the hot sauce and lays them out in the glass dish. I try not to pay attention as I hold the salad spinner tight against me and turn the handle as fast as I can. But I do. She ladles beef onto the sauce, and cheese over it. She works fast, not from efficiency, but annoyance. I failed the test again.

I'm quiet during dinner. In my head I'm working on a new poem. It will begin:

I hear the music and my feet move
All wrong
Jangle Jingle out of step . . .

"So it worked out fine after all," Mom is saying as I
tune back in. "The inspectors came just as my class got
started on our California Missions project. Some of the
kids were making missions out of their sugar cubes; some
were busy on their reports. . . ."

"How about you, Becky-wecky," Dad says. "What's
this I hear about a rabbit?"

My interest perks as Becky tells again about the preschool surprise.

"Remember when Adrienne was her age?" Mom
muses. "She was just as excited about her rabbit." She
laughs in remembrance. "What was its name? Candy?
Sugar? Something like that. Remember, Mark?"

"I remember. And then one day—poof! All of a sudden her interest was gone. She never spoke of it again.
Kids!"

"Marshmallow."

"What?"

"I named the rabbit Marshmallow because it was white
and soft."

"Yes . . . yes . . . that's right. You do remember.
What ever happened to that rabbit, Adrienne?"

I shake my head, puzzled. Until this moment I hadn't
remembered anything about the rabbit. But now I have a
vision of myself in front of some big person, a man, I
think, and he is handing me this wonderfully soft, furry

43

bunny. My heart is thumping with excitement and joy as the warm body fits against my chest, cuddles perfectly into my arms.

So that's how Becky feels today.

"You were such a darling child. So warm and loving, so full of enthusiasm for everything. People would stop us in the street and want to touch your face; you radiated such . . . innocence . . . and joy."

And now? I ask Mom silently. Am I not any of those things now? And if not, why not?

"Yes," Daddy says. "Treehouse was a good school for you. It was good then—and even better now."

"Are you sure?" I ask, surprised to hear the words coming out of me. "How do you know? How can you be really sure?"

There is silence between Mom and Dad and they exchange puzzled glances. Dad breaks the silence with "That's a strange thing to say."

"Yes," Mom picks up. "Do you think we would send you or your sister to anything but the best?"

"Of course not," I say. Mom is angry, and I back down as I usually do.

"Why do you ask that question, Adrienne? Have you any reason to believe Treehouse isn't good?" Dad asks.

"That's ridiculous," Mom answers for me. "Plunkett's been in the preschool business for nineteen years. It's the finest school in the community. There's a two-year waiting list! How can she even ask that question?"

"I don't know, Helen, that's why I'm asking. Adrienne? Was there any *special* reason for your question?"

I think about the little boy this morning, screaming and kicking. I think of the many hours Becky is away from us during the day, under someone else's care. What do we know goes on? And I think about the way Mom described me as a small child—so different from how I am now. I look down at the tightly clasped hands in my lap and say cautiously, "I just wondered. I mean, if preschools are so wonderful for kids, how come that trusting, loving kid you said *I* was grew up into—me?"

Mom gasps. She opens her mouth, then closes it. She looks to Dad for help. Then she says, "What are you talking about? You're a wonderful young woman. You're bright and beautiful, kind, thoughtful, sensitive. You're a wonderful young woman."

Just as always. She denies what I feel. All these nice things she says about me have nothing to do with what I asked—what we know, without ever talking about.

"It's quite normal for teenagers to doubt themselves," Dad says, "but really, sweetheart. You have no reason to put yourself down. People change. I'm certainly not the same person I was at five, or fifteen, or twenty-five."

"I know."

"But back to your original question. What made you ask if we're sure about Becky's school?"

"I don't know. It's just silly, I guess. Now I've wrecked our whole dinner, so let's forget it, okay?"

Becky pokes her finger through a slice of bread and twirls it around. She smiles at me and says, "Wrecker pecker!"

"Becky!" Mom exclaims.

45

Dad frowns while my mouth goes dry. "Ignore her," Dad says quietly. "How about some more coffee, hon?"

Mom nods. She talks about going out Saturday night and asks if I can sit for them. And we're back on safe ground.

Chapter 5

"What are you guys doing Saturday?" Bev asks. We are waiting outside the youth employment office for Ryan and Jason. They check there each day to see if there are any jobs. Ryan's folks say that at seventeen he's too old for an allowance. That if he needs money he should go out and earn it.

"I have to sit Becky," I tell Bev, holding my hands around my eyes so I can see through the glass door to the guys inside. "They've got something. Here they come."

The door swings open and Ryan bounces out, followed by Jason, who punches him playfully on the shoulder. "Hope you have good strong arm muscles," Jason says. "Ever *see* that house? Cathedral windows all across the front. We'll have to squeegee from on top of the bushes. T'ain't gonna be easy, my boy."

Ryan rubs his hands together greedily. "Yeah, but they're paying *forty bucks,* twenty apiece. Not bad!" He puts an arm around me and drawls, "Say, honey chile. You all doin' anything Saturday night?"

"Uh-huh. Gotta sit Becky."

"Aw, *shucks.*" He's only deflated a moment; immediately he says, "No problem. I'll sit with you." He raises and lowers his eyebrows quickly in mock suggestiveness. "*Becky* can chaperone."

"Lucky-y!" Bev exclaims, glancing at Jason. She's wishing no doubt that they could have such a setup. It's always so hard, she often complains, to find a comfortable, warm place to be alone.

"Uhn-uhn. Sorry. Mom won't allow it. You know how she is." I pretend disappointment and feel a little guilty. Mom wouldn't mind a bit.

"Aw, shucks!" Ryan exclaims. "I guess we'll have to make it look legit and invite you guys along too."

"Some chaperones *we'd* make." Jason gives Bev an affectionate squeeze. "Sure. We'll come. For a while, anyway. And then we have other plans."

"Great. Seven thirty, then. Bring a pizza and we'll all share it." We wave good-bye at the school parking lot, but I'm already wondering what I can do to keep Bev and Jason around Saturday so I won't be left alone with Ryan.

Jason zooms past us in his red Pinto and honks good-bye. I glimpse Bev snuggling close to him, arms already around him, and look away.

"They're really something," Ryan says as we walk toward home together. "They're really crazy about each other."

"Yeah." I want to avoid where this subject could lead, so I ask, "Did you hear from Oxie yet?" Ryan wants to study sports medicine and has applied at Occidental College. He's terribly anxious to get in.

48

He doesn't answer right away, and when he does his voice has a bitter edge to it. "Did you ever notice, Adrienne, how you change the subject whenever we get on the subject of closeness?"

"Oh, come on." I dance out in front of him so I'm walking backwards. "Don't be silly. Who's changing the subject? All I did was ask about Oxie."

"You changed the subject."

"I did not! You told me Jason and Bev are crazy about each other and I agreed. What else is there to say?"

"A lot. People who really like each other *show* their feelings. Like *they* do. And us? I'm crazy about you, but you don't let me near you. Don't you think there's something a little weird about our relationship?"

I sober up immediately and fall in step beside him. "I thought you promised not to bring it up again. I thought you said you'd give me more time."

"How *much* more time, Adrienne? A week? A month? A *year?*"

"I don't *know!*"

"Well, at least talk about it. Tell me *why.*"

"Why. Why do I love thee? Let me count the ways."

"It's *how,* and now you're making jokes."

"All right, so I'll be serious. What's to say about closeness?" My heart is thumping with fear I'm going to lose him. Ryan is just like all the other boys. He won't take any more.

"We're still acting like strangers."

"Oh, come on, Ryan," I say, fighting to keep the tears from my voice. "Strangers don't kiss."

"Do you call what we do kissing?"

"Don't *you?*" I hug myself and move away from Ryan so we can't even accidentally touch.

He sighs. "What's the use? If you don't understand, there's no point in explaining it."

"No! *Tell me.*"

We're at the front door to my house now, and he shakes his head sadly as he looks down at me. "It's embarrassing to have to beg. It's obvious you just don't feel the same way I do. I think about you all the time. I lay in bed at night after coming home from seeing you—after a good-night kiss that I always initiate and *you* can barely stand—and I think how wonderful it would be if you cared. I want to hold you and touch your face and kiss you. . . . Oh, what's the use!"

If he would kiss me now I would try, really try to like it. He's the first boy I've gone with that I've *wanted* to love. Is there a gene missing in me that makes me so unloving?

"I don't know what to say." My throat catches.

"Don't say anything."

"It's not your fault, honestly. It's mine. I don't know why I'm this way, and I try not to be."

"Yeah. The trouble is, you shouldn't *have* to try."

For a long moment we stand there, not looking at each other, and I think there has to be something else to say, but I can't think what. "I better go in," I say finally.

"I better be going," he says.

"Will I see you again?" I try not to sound anxious.

"I don't know, Adrienne. I'll have to think about it."

"Oh." I will not let this hurt me; it's happened before.

I will just bury what he said deep in some corner of my brain, where it will never come out. I can even say politely, "See you around, then."

"Yeah." Ryan strides down the walk to the street and walks rapidly away until he disappears around the corner without once looking back. I stare at the empty street and then turn, open the door, and go in.

The house is empty, as it always is when I get home from school. Mom doesn't get back with Becky until nearly five and Dad even later. Usually I like having the house to myself. It gives me time just to "be." I like to go into the kitchen and get an apple, then wander around the house looking out the windows to the trees and mountains and finally go to my room to read or listen to music.

But today it's different. The empty house doesn't give me peace. It only echoes my desolation. I don't want to be alone. I need to talk with someone, keep busy . . . something.

I go into the kitchen, turn on the radio, and look around for work to do. Mom always leaves instructions for dinner on a bulletin board so I can get a start before she gets home. Today we'll have meatloaf surprise. Good. The recipe is rather involved; it will keep my hands busy and my head off Ryan.

I wash my hands and go to the fridge, which is covered with Becky's paintings held on by little magnets in fruit shapes—apples, bananas, pears. Mom adds new paintings almost every day, but I don't think I ever really notice them. Today, though, I stop and look.

Becky's paintings are a cheerful kaleidoscope of reds, yellows, and greens. She paints in big, bold strokes, and I think how free and happy and uninhibited she is.

As I open the refrigerator door, one of those half-formed shadowy scenes that have been bothering me lately flits briefly across my mind. I close my eyes and bite my lip, wanting this time to see more clearly. There is a little girl, perhaps three, painting at an easel. She's wearing a smock—pink, tied at the back—and holding a long-handled paintbrush dripping with black paint. She's shivering, but it can't be cold because there's a bright, strong, almost harsh light, which hurts her eyes, so she must be looking directly into the sun. She . . . she . . . No, *I!* It's me! I'm the little girl! And what's that strange hot smell? And why, in such heat, am I shivering?

As quickly as it came, the scene is gone, and I find myself staring into the interior of the refrigerator without an inkling as to what I'm doing or what the scene means. It's as if time stopped for just that moment. And now, again, I hear the radio. It's Dr. Tony Grant, the psychologist, and she's giving advice to a woman whose husband has asked for a divorce.

I take the package of ground meat, the chunk of cheddar cheese, and an egg from the refrigerator and turn back to stand in the middle of the kitchen, not knowing what to do next. What's going on with me? Am I crazy? Why do I have these strange visions and why do I mess up every boy relationship the way I do? And all of a sudden, I'm crying.

Sunny, Bev's sister, answers the phone. She says that Bev hasn't come home yet and then I realize she must be out still with Jason. I'm so disappointed I nearly start crying all over again.

"Something wrong, Adrienne?" Sunny asks.

"No. Nothing."

"If you want a sympathetic ear, I'm a very good listener and *I'm* home."

"No, no thanks. Please tell Bev I phoned."

"Wait. I think I hear her coming now. Bev?" she calls out. "Telephone! It's Adrienne."

I hear Bev giggling as she comes to the phone, and she says, "Quit it, Jason. Stop that!" Then I hear Sunny whisper that she thinks I've been crying.

If Jason's there, it's a bad time to talk. I want to hang up, but then Bev comes on and her voice is warm and concerned. "What's up, Adrienne? Everything okay?"

"I need to talk to you." I have to stop to blow my nose which always gets stuffed when I cry. "I'm sorry. I forgot you were with Jason."

"He's going home."

"I am not!" I hear Jason cry. "What *is* this?"

Bev must have put her hand over the receiver, because I can't hear what she says next. Then she comes back on. "It's okay, Adri. He just left. He had to . . . uh . . . pick up his mother. I'll be over in ten minutes."

I hang up and stare at the phone and think, *What am I going to say?* I don't even know what's going on myself.

"That's what friends are for," Bev says when I tell her that a few minutes later. "To help sort things out." She rang the bell and when I answer it she takes one look and puts her arms around me. That's all it takes, and I'm off on one great big heaving sob. When I get most of it out, she takes me by the arm and leads me to the bedroom.

I wipe my eyes, smile, and say, "Really, I'm okay now. Let's go down and I'll finish making supper." Restlessly I straighten the papers on my desk, prop up the bedpillows, look out the window. Bev, sitting cross-legged on the floor, watches and finally cries, "Will you settle down! Come on! What's going on?" She gets up, takes me by the shoulders, and pushes me down on the bed. "Now, sit! And talk!"

"Ryan isn't going to see me anymore." I feel the tears start again but hold them back because I need to see Bev's reaction.

She shrugs. "I don't believe it. What happened? You have an argument? So what. You'll make up. He's crazy about you."

"No. Not this time. I don't think so."

She gives me a quizzical look as if she's beginning to see something she hadn't realized before. "Okay, Adri. What's going on? Don't you think it's time you leveled with me?"

And I do. I tell her about all the other boys I've gone out with and why we broke up. I tell her the truth this time, not the excuses I made up when it happened. "The worst of it is, I really like Ryan," I cry. "Really! Until he wants to make out. Then I nearly get . . . sick."

54

Bev watches me, wide-eyed, clearly puzzled; then a strange expression crosses her face. "You're not . . . ?"

"What?" Something about the way she shrinks back makes me realize what she means, and my face gets hot with shame. "No, I'm not a lesbian!"

She looks away, then, as suddenly turns back, a bright smile on her face. "I know! It's hormonal. I just bet! Have you seen a doctor?"

For a second a wave of hope sweeps over me, then reality returns. "It's not hormones. I don't believe that."

"How do you know? How can you be sure? Were you ever checked out?"

I shrug my shoulders, irritably. "I just know it's not. I just know."

"But *how*?"

"Because I *feel* like kissing Ryan. I feel soft and wanting, just the way I should, I guess . . . but then . . . when we do . . . I could puke."

"Oh." Bev takes a deep breath and puts her hand on mine. "Gee, Adri . . . I don't know what to say. I never heard anything like that before. I just don't know what to say."

"What am I going to do?"

"Have you told your mother?"

I shake my head. "And I wouldn't. I couldn't."

We sit there on the rug, facing each other, with nothing more to say. "What am I going to do?" I ask again. "How can I be a woman and hate . . . intimacy?"

Bev shakes her head sadly. "Gee, Adri," she says. "I just don't know. I don't know what to tell you."

Chapter 6

"All right. Now, this is what I've done," Bev says over the phone the next day. "I spoke to Jason about Ryan."

My heart nearly stops. "You didn't! You told Jason? Bev, how could you? What I said was in confidence! Bev!"

"Calm down, Adri. Calm down. I didn't tell him *everything*. You think I'm stupid? I just said the two of you had a fight, and to see if he could do something about it. You know. Just talk to Ryan."

I take a deep, relieved breath and wonder if Ryan will confide in Jason as I have in Bev. It would be so embarrassing to think they'd talk about me—like *that*.

"And Jason just reported back."

I want for her to go on, watching Mom scrub a pot at the sink. I'd been helping clean up after supper when the phone rang. Now, though, the water is running and Becky is chattering next to her; Mom's listening to what I say with her whole body. I turn my back and speak lower.

"You want a blow by blow, or just the bottom line?"

"Bottom line."

"Okay. Jason talked him into spending Saturday night at your house, just the way we planned." Bev sounds triumphant.

Behind me I hear Mom's irritated "Becky! Stop nagging. Good girls do as they're told!"

"How?" I ask softly, turning to see what it is Becky's doing that angers Mom. "How did he talk him into it, and what did Ryan say?"

"Oh, it wasn't all that hard, according to Jase," Bev says. "Apparently Ryan's so stuck on you he just needed a little encouragement, which you, obviously didn't give."

"Did he tell Jason why we argued?" I whisper. Becky has retired to a corner of the kitchen and stands, thumb in mouth, warily watching Mom and looking contrite.

"Now, that's better!" Mom says. "Nobody likes little girls who misbehave!"

Her words rivet my attention, and I feel suddenly as if someone has raked my back with sharp nails. Why must kids be nice to grown-ups, no matter what! How about *children's* feelings? All this stuff about being seen and not heard, about never talking back, about grown-ups knowing what's best . . .

"Adri, you there?"

I take a deep breath and try to concentrate on Bev again.

"Were you listening? Did you hear what I just said?"

"No, sorry. My mind went elsewhere for a sec."

"I said that Ryan told Jase you both decided to cool it for a while."

"Oh."

"Jason's got his own theory, though," she continues. "He thinks the two of you are so thick that you're scared, and that no matter how hard you try to stay apart, *nature* will win out in the end. Which is just what Jason *would* think."

I laugh halfheartedly.

"And you know me. I wouldn't contradict Jase for anything. I said, 'You're probably right.' Is that okay?"

"Perfect. Thanks, Bev. You're a real friend."

"For sure. Now, be smart and do what I told you. Get a checkup. Tell your Mom you have PMS or something— you know, premenstrual syndrome. Then tell the doctor the truth."

"I don't like doctors."

"Oh, Adrienne!" Bev cries. Then she giggles, "You know what? Neither do I."

When we hang up I'm feeling lots better. Bev says they'll all come together around seven thirty, "bearing the biggest, most humongous pizza you ever did see."

I go back to the sink and pick up the dish towel, smiling. Mom asks, "Good news?"

"Uh-huh. I'm going to have company Saturday night while you're out. Bev, Jason, and Ryan."

"How nice." She nods at Becky. "Sweetie . . . get ready for bed."

"Mommy weeed me a stowy?"

"Not tonight, honey. I have too much work to do. But I'll be up later to tuck you in."

"I'll read to her," I say.

"Oh, will you, Adri? Good! Wouldn't you know, just when I'm busiest she has to be especially cranky." Mom impatiently pushes a strand of hair from her face.

"Come on, Becky-wecky, upsy-daisy," I say, going to the corner where she still stands, looking forlorn. I lift her up into my arms, and she nuzzles her face against my cheek, purring with pleasure. She's sucking hard on a thumb, a sure sign that she's very tired or troubled. "I'll read *Peter Rabbit* to you, Becky-wecky. Then, if you want, I'll tell you a story I made up just for you." She snuffles a sigh of contentment and drops her head on my shoulder as I carry her up the stairs to the bedroom.

I feel bad about Becky. It doesn't seem fair that she gets so little attention. She's rushed off to preschool each morning, and when Mom picks her up late in the afternoon she usually has to go along to the market or to other stops Mom has to make before going home. Then, while Mom and I get supper, Becky's put down in front of the TV or at a table with some paper and crayons. And after dinner Becky's pretty much on her own. I usually do homework, after helping clean up, and Mom has all these other things to do before she can sit down for a quiet time with Dad—like laundry and getting bills paid and doing the paperwork for the school where she teaches. You know. And finally, when it's bedtime, Becky's hurried through a bath and into bed and through a quick story, and that's that.

It must have been that way for me, too, when I was little, though I don't remember. And it's sad.

Tonight, because I'm thinking these things, I feel especially protective and tender toward my little sister. I start a warm bath and help her undress.

"And how's Peter Rabbit today?" I ask, lifting her shirt —with its three overlapping hearts down its front—over her head. I expect a smile, but instead she yawns a deep, overtired, almost tearful yawn.

"Did you feed her today?"

"Nope."

"How come?" I pull down her jeans and help her out of them. Her panties are wet. Oh, boy. I thought she'd outgrown accidents.

She unplugs the thumb from her mouth just long enough to say, "Andwea got to feed her today."

"Oh?" I pull off the wet pants and wonder if I should tell Mom about them. "Why's that? I thought she was *your* bunny."

She seems to be struggling over how to answer my question and finally says, "Andwea's a *good* girl."

"Oh, well. So are you!"

Becky stares back at me with solemn, guarded eyes and I wonder if she was punished for wetting her pants or if she wet her pants because she was punished.

"You know what?" I pick her up to carry her to the tub. "You tell me who said you weren't good and I'll punch him right in the shnozzola!" I push my finger against her nose, then rub noses until she giggles.

She's more interested in playing in the tub than in the questions I ask about her school day, so I just let her be. One minute she's zooming a toy boat around the water, calling out rhymes: boat goat, dope hope. The next minute she talks about the bad little girl on the boat who she's going to teach a lesson. And she sinks the boat.

"Now why did you go and do that?" I ask, soaping the satin-smooth skin of her back. "The little girl will drown."

"Good," she says with satisfaction. And I can't imagine my sweet little sister being so vicious. I give her a playful swat as I lift her from the tub to wrap in a thick terry towel and say, "I think this little girl is angry because she's very tired, so off to bed. And I bet *tomorrow* you'll get to feed Peter Rabbit. Okay?"

"Okay," she says sweetly, trustingly, and she plugs her thumb back into her mouth. "Now tell Becky a stowy."

It's nearly seven thirty, Saturday night, and I can't keep my eyes off the clock. I'm wearing new jeans and a light green sweater, Ryan's favorite color. I guess I'm too anxious to give Becky my usual attention because she's particularly demanding and begs to stay up later. "Just till Wyan comes."

And now the bell rings. My stomach churns, my heart pounds loudly, and my hands get clammy.

"I'll get it!" Becky cries, racing for the door. I run after her because you never know who she'll open to.

Someone is pounding on the door. "Hey in there! Hurry up! Pizza's getting cold!" It's Jason's booming voice, and Bev is giggling, telling him to stop it or he'll knock a hole in the wood. No sound from Ryan. Is he with them?

61

For a second I hold still, trying to catch my breath, trying to gather myself together to appear unconcerned. And then I open the door.

"Make way for Mr. Pizza Man!" Jason calls, invading the room with his presence. He marches straight for the kitchen. Bev, arm linked through his, winks and shrugs.

Ryan enters behind them. We barely make eye contact, but in the brief time we do, I sense he's as shy and uncertain as I and maybe even more guarded.

Fortunately Becky eases things. She latches onto Ryan and pulls him into the family room, where I've set up the table with cola and apple juice, a big salad and a platter of chocolate chip cookies.

"Look what Wyan bwought!" Becky cries, tugging at my sweater. "Adwi, look!"

She's holding a small, beautifully illustrated, and old copy of *Peter Rabbit*. It looks as if it might even be a rare edition, and I glance questioningly at Ryan.

"It's nothing," he says. "It was one of the first books I ever owned. Some relative gave it—you know—and she's so crazy about rabbits that I thought, well—you know."

A tear springs to my eye at his thoughtfulness, but I avoid looking at him. "Have you thanked Ryan, honey?" I ask, stooping to Becky's eye level to see the book.

She glances up at Ryan and smiles brightly. Then she throws her arms around his legs and buries her face against his body.

"Hey, hey," Ryan says, obviously embarrassed. He lifts her and gives her a hug. But then Becky does something that turns me to ice. She bends back, looks Ryan soulfully in the eyes, then kisses him on the mouth—tongue out.

"Becky!" I gasp, glancing around to see if the others have noticed. Bev is frowning and Jason laughs. Ryan turns a deep shade of pink and puts Becky down very quickly.

"Man!" Jason exclaims. "That sister of yours is going to be one hot number in ten years."

"Don't be gross," Bev says.

"Bedtime," I say brightly. "Come on, sweetie. Say good-night." I take Becky's hand and lead her away, but every cell in my body is trembling. Where did she learn to kiss like that? Surely, not from *our* family! We always kiss on the cheek. From TV?

"What took you so long? We're starved!" Jason complains when I get back to the living room. He clutches his stomach as if he can't wait another minute.

"Okay, okay," Bev soothes, patting him on the head. She joins me in the kitchen at the microwave. "Stop worrying," she whispers as we wait for the pizza to re-heat. "It's going to be okay. The guys have been talking about school and teachers ever since you left."

"How could she do that? It was so gross!" I exclaim.

"Aw, forget it. Kids do funny things sometimes. My mother caught my baby brother eating his own doo-doo once."

"You're kidding!"

"Honestly."

"His BM?"

She nods. And then both of us start laughing.

Between slices of hot, sweet-smelling pepperoni and cheese pizzas, we all talk. First about silly things. Then about the possibility of nuclear war. Ryan says, with the Soviets and Americans building more and more bombs, there's got to be a war one day. "Did you ever hear of any weapon invented that wasn't eventually used?" he asks.

"What can *we* do?" I ask.

"That's easy," Jason answers. "Live for today. Tomorrow may never come."

"Oh, *Jase!*" Bev cries in disgust. "Don't start that!"

"Oh, yeah? Well, I think these guys ought to think about it. They're in love. They're crazy for each other. Why wait? How do they know what tomorrow will bring?"

"The world's not going to end tomorrow!" Bev looks from me to Ryan apologetically. "Quit it, Jase." But Jason is only warming up.

"I know just how you guys feel. We feel the same. Only it's crazy not to see each other just because you might go too far."

"Jason! It's none of our business!" Bev cries. "Shut . . . up!"

Ryan seems to have drawn into a shell. He has a strained, distracted expression on his face, and I feel as if all the blood in my body has congealed in my chest. That Jason is such a clod! How can Bev stand him?

"I know what. Let's play Monopoly," Ryan says.

"Nah. Let's put on some music and dance," Jason replies.

Bev starts clearing the table. "Why don't you get the Monopoly set, Adri?"

"Okay, okay," Jason says finally. "I get the point. Monopoly it is." He starts to help Bev and Ryan pick up the pizza litter while I go for the Monopoly set.

Though the game starts under a strain, it develops into a fun two hours. Jason, as banker, likes to steal the money and likes to get caught. Bev is a hard-nosed dealer when it comes to trading properties, and Ryan is lucky and lands on some of the best lots. We call it quits when it looks like a draw between Ryan and Bev, because Jason is getting restless. "Hey, let's go, Bev. It's getting late."

"Do you mind, Adri?" Bev asks. She's wondering, of course, if I want to be alone with Ryan.

"Well, I guess I better go too," Ryan says, still avoiding my eyes. Maybe he's waiting for me to urge him to stay, but I don't.

I stand up as Bev goes for her sweater. Ryan stays at the table sorting some of the play money, but as soon as Bev and Jason go to the door, he does too. For one awkward moment we all stand facing each other, the three of them on one side, me on the other.

"Thanks for coming," I say. "My folks should be home soon, and it was fun having you. And thanks, too, for the *Peter Rabbit* book, Ryan."

He nods. His eyes are expressionless. It's as if he has lost all feeling for me.

"Well, so long. See you in school Monday!" I close the door after them and relax the smile I have fixed on my lips. I am so tired, so very tired.

Chapter 7

I sit on my bed writing. Not in the book Ryan gave me. That's for copying only the best poems and thoughts. My journal is a black and white notebook in which I write bits of things I hear at home or at school; word pictures—of a sunset, a flower with dew on it; sometimes a whole page on what it's like when the bell rings at school and we all rush out into the halls: the noise, the smells, the movement. Sometimes I just write a paragraph about something that touches me.

Today I am putting down—or trying to—*feelings*. Those are the hardest to describe, because I tend to edit the truth in case someone should read my journal sometime. Now I write:

I hardly see R anymore. I go through the school day waiting for each period to end so that maybe, in those few minutes between classes, we'll pass. It's amazing how, when we *were* seeing each other, he was everywhere. But now it's as if he's disappeared from the face of the earth.

Yesterday I went looking for him. I didn't know

what I'd say if I actually found him, but I wanted to put myself where we could at least pass. Maybe something would happen. So when the bell rang after French, I hurried out of the room and joined the growing mobs moving along the hall.

R's geometry class is only four doors away. When we were seeing each other he'd rush from his room to pick me up at French, and then we'd walk on together to my next class.

When I reached his room the kids were streaming out like water through a funnel, and for a while I had to stand aside. Some kids knew me and nodded. One said, "Looking for R? He's inside."

The crowd finally thinned and I peered into the room. The only people left were the teacher and R, or so I thought at first. His back was to me and a happy-scared tremor rushed through me. But then he moved, and I saw someone else was there. He was talking with a pretty blond girl who glanced my way and smiled, then returned her attention to R.

Before he could see me I turned and ran.

I go through the days like a robot, pretending everything's fine. No one, not even Bev, knows how empty I feel.

"Adri?" It's Dad. "Got a minute?"

I hurriedly push my journal under the pillow and pull out a schoolbook. "Sure. Come in," I call out.

Dad strides into the room, looking around as if he's in a strange country and everything is different. "Hi, honey.

Your mother seems to think I've been neglecting you. She thinks we ought to have a little chat."

Oh, oh. Mom noticed that Ryan isn't coming around anymore and she can't handle asking me directly, so she's sent the second in command. "What about?" I ask, moving over so Dad can sit down.

"Oh, just things . . . how everything's going with you." He takes my hand in his big one, covering it with his other hand so I can't pull away. "You seem a little sad lately. Withdrawn. Things going okay at school?"

"Sure, Dad. I'm doing fine."

"How's that nice young man you were seeing—Ryan?"

"Fine."

Dad clears his throat. "I haven't seen him around the last few weeks. Anything wrong?"

"Oh, no. We just had a little disagreement."

There's a long pause while Dad studies me intently. I ease my hand out of his and look away. "Adri, honey," he says at last, "Mother seems to think you have some kind of problem relating to boys. You want to talk about it?"

"No!"

"Oh. Why not?"

"Because it won't change anything."

Dad doesn't answer immediately, but then he says, "What do you want to change?"

"I don't know! How I feel! How Mom listens! She doesn't listen. She never did! She doesn't listen to Becky either!"

"Oh, come now, Adri. That's not fair. Your mother

tries very hard. She has a lot of pressure with a job and family and all. She tries her best."

"Oh, sure!" I clench my jaws because it's really true, what Dad says. I shouldn't be so hard on her. How can I blame the way I am on anyone, except myself?

He takes my hand again, and I'm embarrassed because it's damp and cold. "What is it she doesn't hear, Adrienne? What is it you're wanting to say or Becky's saying —that you think she doesn't hear?"

"Well, like . . . like . . ." Of all the possible examples I might cite the one that comes rushing from my mouth surprises me. "Like . . . when I was little . . . Becky's age . . . and didn't want to go to school." I start shivering and hug my arms around myself. All the old anger and fear is back and I feel three again. "I begged. I cried! But did she listen? No!"

Dad takes me by the shoulders and looks directly into my eyes. "That's a very strange example to bring up now, after all these years, isn't it?"

"Why? Why *didn't* she listen?" I persist. "She didn't! She never listens!"

"Adri, honey. Lots of small children cry about going off to preschool. They don't like being separated from their mothers. That's what preschool is for, to help them become less dependent so they can eventually go to regular school without problems. Now, what's this all about?"

Of course he's right, and I don't know why that particular example is so important that I'm still shaking. "I don't *know* . . ."

Dad studies me for a long time and scratches his beard. "I don't understand why you're harboring so much resentment, honey. Your mother doesn't deserve it. She loves you and always has. She wishes you could be more open with her. She really wants that; surely you know. Will you try?"

I nod, agreeing, but I think even he reads the truth. There's no way I could ever confide in Mom.

"Now," Dad says. "Is there some way you can patch things up with this boyfriend? He seems such a nice young man. Surely, if you talk out what it is you disagreed about . . ."

I shake my head vigorously. "No, I don't think so. I think he's seeing someone else already."

"Oh." Dad touches my cheek and smiles. "No matter. You're young. There will be lots of good men in your life. You're a lovely, bright, loving young woman. So wipe the tears from those pretty eyes and come inside. Mother is making popcorn and hot chocolate for us."

"In a minute."

Dad nods. He gets up, pats me on the head, says "Don't be too long," and leaves the room.

I sit cross-legged on my bed, staring at the closed door. It was good to explode like that, even though nothing was resolved. But Daddy doesn't know me any better than Mom does. Or how could he have ever called me "loving"?

"You're not loving? Boy, can you be dense!" Bev says a few days later while we're walking through the shopping

70

mall together. "I never knew anyone as caring and loving as you. Just look how you are with Becky. And me."

"You know what I mean."

"I sure do, and you surprise me, Adri. I thought you were smart. Just because you don't do a lot of hugging and kissing . . . Well, look at Jason. He's great with that sort of thing, but I can't exactly call him 'caring' or 'loving.' "

"Then why do you go with him?"

She gives me a sheepish grin. "He's a gorgeous hunk and a challenge to keep in line—not that I usually want to keep him in line."

"You really *like* sex, don't you?"

"Mmmm!" Now she smiles very sweetly. "He makes me feel *wonderful,* all soft and yet on fire. When we're together my mind goes absolutely blank . . . and I just *feel.*"

"I wish I could be that way."

She puts an arm around my waist and gives me a squeeze. "I wish it too. And you will. Have you seen that doctor yet?"

"No."

She squeezes me again, but not affectionately. "Well . . . do!"

For a while we walk along, stopping in front of window displays and peering in, talking about styles, or not talking at all. Actually my mind is only half with her. The thought of seeing a doctor triggers some unpleasant feelings. Stethoscopes, cold, on my chest. Quick, painful shots in an arm or hip. Thumpings, proddings. And all

71

the while smiles of assurance and denial. "Now, that didn't really hurt, did it? Big girls don't cry!"

Even in recent years, when I go for the annual checkup, I dread going and worry for days in advance.

Doctors. Playing doctor. A scene flickers brightly for an instant, then fades. I am small and naked and where is Mommy? Why do they touch me? I don't like these hands, those faces so close. Hard things hurting. Why doesn't Mommy come? Why doesn't she stop them?

"What's wrong, Adri? You're shivering!" Bev says. "And you look so—strange."

We are standing before a lingerie display and I am back in the shopping mall. I take a deep, ragged breath. "I just had the weirdest memory, or dream, I don't know which. Did you ever play doctor when you were young?"

"Oh, did I!" Bev laughs and covers her mouth to whisper. "My older cousins used to get us younger kids together whenever there was a family gathering. They'd pretend we were patients and they were the doctors. We'd have to undress, of course." She rolls her eyes.

"Was it fun?"

"Scary and exciting and, yes, fun. We just *knew*, even though nobody ever said so, that the grown-ups would throw fits if they found out."

"That's funny, because I can't remember any feelings like that, only being scared and feeling pain."

"I don't know why you felt pain. We took temperatures and pretended to give shots, but . . ." She gazes questioningly at me.

"Let's not talk about it anymore. It gives me goose bumps. I feel just rotten."

"Well . . . okay . . ." Bev says. We both turn back to the window display, but it's a while before anything comes into focus. "What do you think of that black bikini?" I ask, trying to show Bev that everything's okay now.

She cocks her head and frowns, studying the mannequin for a second. "My honest opinion?"

"Absolutely."

"If I wore something like that Jason's eyes would pop right out and then he'd salivate and then he'd tear it off me in one second flat!"

We both laugh, and I'm so glad to have Bev for a friend. She puts all my silly fears into perspective. I file away the thought that I might ask Bev sometime just how far she's gone with Jason. And how far she's willing to go.

Chapter 8

Maybe Bev is right about my problem being hormones. Wouldn't it be terrific if all it took was a couple of shots of estrogen and I'd be just like everyone else? Maybe those weird mental flashes are caused by that, and those shots will make them stop.

Without telling anyone, I phone for an appointment to see Dr. Warner, Bev's family doctor. I give the reception-ist a false name, because I wouldn't want her calling home or sending any bills to the house. And when I check in at the doctor's office, I'm almost shaking with fear that someone might recognize me.

"Gail Green?" the receptionist asks as I stand at the window of the waiting room.

I nod. Though I have rehearsed my false name a dozen times, it still sounds strange to me.

"Will you fill this out, please."

She gives me a pen and clipboard with a sheet on it. There are questions such as name and address, insur-ance coverage, responsible relative, former illnesses, drug reactions. I sit down and fill in only my false name

74

and fake address. Across the room a young mother with two small, squiggly children smiles at me, then goes back to entertaining them.

"You didn't answer all the questions," the receptionist says, taking the clipboard from me.

"It's because I'm not sick," I say in a whisper. "I just want to talk with the doctor. And I'll be paying cash."

The plump woman behind the window looks more closely at me. I can almost read her mind. "Here's another teenager wanting birth control devices."

"Well, all right. Just sit down and we'll call you."

It's a small room and you can hear what anyone says. I take the same chair, across from the young mother and a middle-aged woman with an elderly man. The children eye me as if, with the slightest encouragement, they'd be at my side, but I don't want company. My hands are clammy and my throat is dry and every minute seems an hour. I pluck the nearest magazine from the table—*Better Homes and Gardens*—and open its pages without seeing.

"Gail Green."

For a second I gaze around the room waiting for someone to stand, then realize it's me she's calling. I jump up and follow the nurse down a long hall to a small room with a sink, an examining table, and a chair. She hands me a blue paper gown. "Put this on and the doctor will be with you in a moment," she says, showing me how it unfolds.

I clutch the gown, almost paralyzed with uncertainty, and finally blurt out that I'd like to see the doctor first. She hesitates. "What's the problem?"

I'm not used to standing up to adults, or insisting on my way, and I can feel my face flame with embarrassment. "I'd rather tell the doctor," I say softly.

She nods and opens the door to leave. "He'll be with you in a few minutes." She drops the clipboard on the examining table, its long white paper sheet crackling under the weight.

The room is cold. Not just physically. It's so undecorated. Except for a calendar on the beige and white checked wallpaper there is nothing that isn't white or chrome. I pace back and forth the length of the little cell, eyeing the examining table with distrust, wishing I'd never come. At last the door opens again and the doctor, a man of about fifty with a reddish beard and thinning hair, comes in. He picks up the clipboard, glances at it, and says, "Hello, Gail. Why don't you sit down. And what can I do for you?"

I sit on the chair. He perches on the edge of the examining table, arms crossed, watching me.

"Well, I . . ." I stop, not knowing where to begin.

"Go on. I don't bite."

"It's just very hard to explain. I thought you might want to recommend some estrogen or something." I look up, hopefully.

"Are you not having your menstrual cycle yet?"

"What? No, no. My periods are regular. That's not it at all!"

"Well, then, why don't you tell me what *is* bothering you?"

I clutch my hands between my legs and look down at the plain beige carpeting. I've got to tell, somehow.

Dr. Warner echoes my last words. "You're afraid to get close? How close?" He bends the corner of my questionnaire sheet up and back, up and back, until I'm sure it will tear. "You have a right to feel uncomfortable about intimacy when you're not ready for it. That's good sense."

"But . . ." I feel the tears flood my eyes. "I can't even stand someone I really like holding me, kissing me!"

The doctor's gray eyes show no expression.

"Couldn't you give me some hormone shots? Wouldn't that cure me?"

"I'm afraid not."

"Why?"

"Nothing you've said indicates hormonal imbalance."

"But it has to!" When he doesn't answer, I ask, "Then what do I do?"

He thinks for a second. "Are your parents very strict, perhaps? Have they ever talked about sex . . . made you feel, perhaps that it's wrong, or dirty . . ."

"Oh, no! Not at all!"

"Have you talked with them about it? You'd be surprised how understanding they might be. And just getting it out in the open . . ."

"No!"

"Ummm. Well, I'll tell you, Gail. I think you're making a mountain out of a molehill. Maybe you just haven't met the boy you care enough about."

I look down again.

"Listen, child. I know, at your age, it seems an enormous problem, but believe me, you're better off being selective. Some youngsters who come to me don't know how to say no. I've had girls pregnant at twelve."

"Can't you do *any*thing?"

He takes a prescription pad from a pocket in his white coat, which for a second gives me hope. Then he says, "I recommend a therapist. If you feel this strongly, perhaps she would be helpful." He scribbles as he talks, rips off a sheet, and hands it to me. "If you're really bothered, go see her. She deals exclusively with adolescent problems." He stands, signaling that we're through, and opens the door, holding it for me to come out. By the time I'm in the hall he's striding away. "Well, Mr. Shaw," I hear him say as he opens another door, "and how is that bursitis today?"

I leave thirty-five dollars with the receptionist, dollars earned from baby-sitting jobs and extra chores around the house, and hurry home.

The screams from Becky's room start around ten o'clock. I am just finishing my nightly journal entry when it begins—an eerie wail first, then shrieks of terror.

Dressed only in my nightgown I dash into the hall, almost bumping into Mom, who charges by, flings open the door, and switches on the light.

Becky doesn't even see us. She's sitting up in bed, wide awake, clutching her bedclothes and cowering. I glance to the window, almost expecting to see an intruder, but of course there is no one.

"What is it, sweetie? What's wrong?" Mom coos, wrapping Becky in her arms. "What's my sweetie crying about?"

Rigid, Becky doesn't reply. She just points to the window as if something's there and keeps screaming.

"Becky! Wake up!" Mom cries, shaking her lightly. "Come on, honey. It's just a bad dream." To me she adds, "She seems to be hallucinating."

"Can I do anything? Get her a glass of water?"

"I don't think so. *Becky!* Come on, darling. Wake up!"

For a while I watch, feeling helpless, then I, too, try to reach her. "Becky. Becky, honey," I call softly, putting my face in the path of whatever is frightening her. "It's Adri. What's out there? What's scaring you?"

Her eyes never waver, don't even blink, and the look of horror remains. But this time she says, "Wabbit!"

"Rabbit?" I look up at Mom. "How can she be afraid of a rabbit?" I turn back to Becky. "Where is it, honey?"

"Wabbit!" She screams and points to the top of the drapes.

"There's no rabbit there, honey," Mom says. "You're just dreaming." Mom puts her palm over Becky's forehead, checking for fever.

"Becky!" I say very loud. "Watch me now. I'm going to take the rabbit off those drapes and throw him outside. Okay?"

For a second I think Becky hears me.

"Now watch, honey. See? Come on, rabbit! Get off that drape. This is Becky's room. Come on, outside with you!"

Mom gives me an appreciative, comprehending nod. I

stretch high up, pretend to tug at the invisible rabbit, and keep talking. "Bad rabbit! How dare you frighten my sister! Come with me!" Grabbing the imaginary animal by its imaginary ears, I walk briskly past Mom and Becky and out the bedroom door. I march down the hall to the front door, open it, wait a second, and say, "There! Bad rabbit is gone!" And I slam the door as hard as I can.

When I come back to the room Becky is in Mom's arms, whimpering, but no longer so terrorized. Her eyes are closed, and Mom lays her back in bed, kisses her, and with a finger to her lips, tiptoes out, flipping the light switch.

Without a word I follow her into the living room, where Dad has slept through it all with the TV on. Mom drops down into a chair. "I wonder what's going on. She came home terribly tired today and she's been really out of sorts. And destructive. I don't know what's gotten into her. She wants to tear up everything in the house."

"Maybe something happened at Treehouse," I say.

"Maybe. Maybe they took the rabbit away. You know how much it meant to her. I haven't heard her talk about it for a while now. Or maybe she's coming down with something. When you were that age, you caught every bug that was going around." Mom reaches for a stack of papers on the nearby table and picks up a pencil. "You had nightmares at that age too. Fairy tales are full of violence and cruelty, and Becky's a sensitive child." She sighs. "I'll speak with Martha Plunkett tomorrow." She bends over the papers and starts marking them. For a while I watch, then say, " 'Night, Mom."

She looks up, and there are dark shadows under her eyes and a preoccupied frown between the brows. " 'Night, honey. That was quick of you to play along with Becky. It never occurred to me. I wish they'd never given that animal to her. I remember when yours died."

"*Died?*" I feel weak and lean on the chair opposite Mom.

"Oh, yes. You must have been Becky's age, and you were just crazy about it. It's all you could talk about for weeks . . . and then, suddenly, nothing. I didn't notice at first. And when I asked you weeks later . . . all you said was that the rabbit died."

"How?"

"You never did give me a clear answer."

A bottled-up poison begins to fizz through my whole body, so sickening I can barely stand it. And somehow I know the rabbit has something to do with it, the way I feel toward Mom, the way I feel about boys.

I try, really try, to bring that rabbit into focus. Marshmallow? It must have been white, maybe with long, soft rabbit ears like pictures I've seen. I repeat the name again and again but no image springs to life.

"Maybe it died of old age. Or maybe one of the kids hurt it and it had to be put to sleep," I say. "Kids aren't too gentle with animals sometimes, you know."

"Maybe." Mom's eyes remain on my face for a while, and then she says, "Well, I better get to these papers. I promised the kids I'd return them tomorrow. Goodnight, honey."

" 'Night."

"And thanks."

Thanks. For talking with her all of two minutes? I really am a witch!

Though I climb into bed when I get back to my room, I can't sleep. I think again of Becky and try to remember what Treehouse was like for me at her age, but everything gets tangled. Unable to sleep, I decide to get down the journal Ryan gave me. It has been days since I fingered its butter-soft leather or read any of the entries, and maybe it would give me comfort and pleasure.

Climbing on the desk chair, I check the shelf where I'd placed it when Becky was in my room, but it isn't there. I think hard. Where could it be? My desk where I used to keep it, maybe?

But it's not there either. An uneasy feeling creeps through me. I can't have lost it. I never took it out of the room. *Would Mom?* No! I check my dresser drawers, under my bed, on the window ledge, and then, suddenly, I see it. It's on the floor between my bed and the wall. I'm annoyed at my carelessness. I must have been reading it on the bed and fallen asleep and it dropped off. Now that smooth, fine leather will be scratched.

Still, I can't recall . . .

I pick up the book and examine the cover. Everything seems okay. Then I open it to the first page.

I cry out. The endpaper is covered with black, scrawling crayon marks. So is the first page and the next and next. Every page I have written on has been defaced with some kind of mark—a cross, squiggly lines, jagged lines, meaningless scribbles in blacks and dark greens and browns.

"Oh, Becky," I cry. "Why?" And then, sobbing, I run into the living room to Mom.

Chapter 9

"It has to be Becky! Who else could it be?" I am kneeling in front of Mom showing her the horrible scribbles.

"What? What's wrong?" Dad wakes, disoriented, clicks the remote to turn off the TV, and comes to us.

"You could cut these pages out, if you do it very carefully, so it wouldn't hurt the binding," Mom muses. "You could copy over the poems on other sheets." She turns the pages slowly, frowning.

"But what about the endpapers?" My throat aches with tears. Even the endpapers—the heavy pages glued to the book covers on the inside and to the first and last pages—have been ruined. They had been so beautiful, shaded, like moiré, in a soft green that complemented the deep red leather. I feel sick, like I could throw up. I want to run back to my room and just pull the covers over my head and scream. How could Becky do that?

"Maybe we could take it to a bookbinder, have new endpapers put in," Mom suggests.

Dad puts his hand on my head. "I don't think so, Helen. The book just wouldn't be the same for Adri." He strokes my head, and the kindness is too much. I cover my face and start to cry.

Mom puts the book aside and leans over to hug me, but I pull away, stand up, and stumble out of the room. "Adrienne, honey!" Mom calls. But I can't stay.

Ten minutes later I am lying on my bed curled up, eyes wide open, staring at the wall, when there is a knock.

"Honey? May we come in? We'd like to talk to you."

I don't answer, and the door opens anyway. Mom and Dad come to the bed and sit down, turning to me.

"It's a terrible thing, what Becky did," Dad says. "But you must remember, she's a very little girl."

"Nevertheless," Mom says sternly, "it was wrong. And Becky must have *known* it was wrong. She should be punished."

"Did you do anything that might have set her off?" Dad asks. "Could she have any reason—not that there could be *any* justification—but in her child's mind . . ."

"I didn't do *anything!*" I cry, sitting up suddenly.

"I just don't understand," Mom says. "She's always been such a sweet child. She's never done anything like this before."

"She's changed! Don't you see it?"

"Changed. How?" Dad glances at Mom. "What do you mean?"

"She wets her pants lately, and she hasn't done that in a long time!"

"Yes, that's true," Mom says. "I've been worrying about it. In fact one day last week she came home with a different pair of panties on, and when I asked Plunkett the next day she said it was because Becky wet herself at school."

"Maybe you should take her to the doctor," Dad suggests.

"Maybe I should."

"But it's not only that!" I say. "She was playing with some of her stuffed animals yesterday and talking to herself—you know, how she does—and she told this gruesome story about how the lion bit the dog's head off, then smashed its body against a rock. It was just so full of violence, I got the shivers."

"Helen?" Dad asks.

Mother is silent a moment, then says, "I think it's the age. I remember reading in the book I have on the three-year-old that the stories they tell are often about people hurting others . . . animals dying . . . that sort of thing. I'm almost sure."

"But . . . but . . ." I sputter. I know there is something wrong, but I can't put my finger on it. And I can see by the expression on Mom's face that she's talking herself out of believing anything is wrong.

"But what?" Dad asks.

"Three weeks ago . . . when Ryan was here . . . she kissed him . . . on the lips."

Dad is unimpressed.

"It wasn't only that. She had . . . she put . . ." I feel my face begin to burn. "She put her . . . tongue in his mouth."

"Oh, *Adrienne!*" Mom exclaims in disgust. "I don't believe that! You must be mistaken!"

86

"I'm not! I'm not! The others saw too—Bev and Jason— We talked about it later!"

"Well she couldn't have learned it in *this* house!"

Dad is thoughtful for a moment, then says, "Did you ask why she did it?"

"I did. And she just clammed up. She looked at me as if she didn't even understand what I was talking about."

"Has she done it since?"

"No. At least as far as I know."

"Well, there," Mom says. "It's best not to make an issue over that kind of behavior. Sometimes it's just a means of getting attention. The less said, the better."

"Aren't you going to say anything to her about what she did to my book?" Just referring to it brings the tears back.

"Of course, Adri. And she's never to go into your room again without permission or she'll be punished."

"Then you don't think there's something wrong?"

Mom puts a consoling hand on my arm. "I don't think so, dear, but we'll all be especially watchful from now on. And the first chance I get I'll have a real talk with Martha Plunkett."

"We're sorry about the book, Adri. Maybe we can find another just like it," Dad offers.

I shake my head. It wouldn't mean the same.

"Well, it's late. Better get to bed now. And Adri . . . be gentle with Becky. I'm sure she didn't know what she was doing."

Mom and Dad leave the room and turn off the light. For a moment I see them together, Dad's arm around

Mom's shoulder, silhouetted in the doorway. They each call good-night to me, and then the door closes. And I lay in my bed for a long time thinking about it all and wondering what, if anything, I can do.

The next day as I'm leaving English, my thoughts totally on Becky and what happened yesterday, someone calls my name. It's Craig, the boy who sits near me in class and often shares my texts because he forgets his own. He's a happy guy; always telling jokes. I don't know how he remembers them all; I can't even recall the really good ones two minutes after hearing them.

"Say, Adrienne," he says, falling into step beside me. "If you're not busy Saturday night, want to go out? There's a good show at the Hastings."

The news must be around that I'm no longer seeing Ryan. It's weeks now. I suppose I should try again. But do I like Craig enough to bother? No. I just can't face going through the whole thing all over again. Maybe I was cut out to be a nun. Maybe I should go into a convent.

"Thanks, Craig, but I . . . can't." It's better than lying that I have something else doing, but it's not as good as coming right out and saying "Thanks, and please don't ask me again."

His face goes blank and I think it must be hard on guys to be turned down, so I try to soften his disappointment. "It's really nice of you to ask, though."

"Yeah. Well, another time," he says peeling off and heading down the hall in the opposite direction.

My next class is French, and habit turns my thoughts to

Ryan. In the past he would always be standing outside my room, waiting, and a sense of hopeful expectation races through me for a second, until I remind myself that he doesn't do that now. So I cross the courtyard separating the French and English rooms, noting the couples holding hands and even embracing or kissing, and smile at kids who greet me. How little I show on the outside of how I really feel.

Into another building and around a corner and I am passing Ryan's geometry class, peering anxiously ahead to see if, maybe, *maybe,* he's waiting. And then, unexpectedly, he comes out of geometry and there he is right in front of me.

Without warning my eyes well up with tears. He's wearing a red plaid wool shirt over a red T-shirt and his patched jeans. Every one of the dozen or more patches he personally sewed on himself, and the jeans are a work of art.

"Hi," he says softly.

"Hi," I reply, suddenly at a loss for words.

"How've you been?"

"Fine."

"How's Becky? Did she like that Peter Rabbit book I brought?"

I hesitate. Should I tell him the truth, that she doesn't want me to read it to her? I say, "Things are sort of strange with her."

"Strange? How?"

"It's a long story."

We stand facing each other as kids flow by into the

classroom, and I can tell he feels hurt that I don't want to say more, so I add, "She crayoned all over that beautiful book you gave me!" I can hardly get the words out.

The only thing I had left of Ryan was that book and now I don't even have that.

"Oh, gee, Adri, I'm really sorry." Ryan almost touches me, but withdraws his hand at the last moment.

"Hi, Ryan! Coming in?" It's the pretty blond girl I saw him with a few weeks ago. She touches his arm possessively.

"In a minute," he says.

"That's all right, Ryan. I have to go anyway. See you." I hurry off to my classroom four doors away before he can see the tears.

One of the things I miss most since Ryan and I broke up is being with Bev. When Ryan and I went together, we often did things with her and Jason. Now, since Bev spends most of her spare time with Jase, I don't see nearly as much of her as I'd like.

Today, though, we arrange to meet. She has something to ask me, to get my opinion on, she explains with unusual self-consciousness. Will I meet her after school and walk home with her?

We live near each other in what's called the Foothills because the homes are at the foot of the hills. It's been especially warm and sunny since the new year, and spring has come early. The air is fragrant with the scent of mock orange, and the colors pull the eye everywhere —to the slopes where carpets of brilliant orange and purple ice plant blaze, to the nearby gardens bright with daffodils and daisies. The birds line the telephone wires like spectators at a show or swoop around in dangerous mating games.

For a while, as we stroll along Journey's End, we talk of school and friends. I pick some strands of purple lantana growing wild through a fence and add it to my small bouquet.

When Bev hears about my visit to the doctor she says, "Why *don't* you see a therapist? He's probably right." And I mumble some kind of nothing that doesn't commit me to anything.

About Ryan she reluctantly admits that he's dating Susan, the blond girl, but that she's really not the least important to him. Of course she couldn't possibly know, but it's kind of her to say it.

Bev seems unusually preoccupied as we walk, as if she's mulling something over and hasn't decided yet how to bring it out. I've seen her this way before and know there's no use in pushing.

Finally she says, "You're my best friend, right?"

"Right." Her voice has dropped an octave, a clear sign that she's very anxious. Not wanting to spook her, I don't even look her way.

"And we've always shared secrets, as long as we've known each other. Right?"

"Right."

"Well, I want to tell you something that you must promise, you must absolutely *swear*, never to tell anyone."

"My goodness. You've got me very curious. What's happened? Are your parents getting a divorce?" I smile at her, because it's the last thing that's likely to happen. Bev's parents still celebrate events like Valentine's Day with romantic dinners or weekends away.

"Adrienne, don't make jokes. This is very serious. And I need your opinion."

"Okay, so shoot."

"First, promise."

I hold up the hand with the flowers as if I'm swearing to an oath in court. "I, Adrienne Meyer, do solemnly swear to keep secret whatever my friend Beverly Crowder tells me till death us do part."

"All right," Bev says, giving me an anxious smile. "Let's sit down."

We sit on a low garden wall along the private street with an olive tree behind us. The ground is littered with squashed olives.

Staring at her feet, Bev says, "Jason's pressuring me to —to have sex with him. What do you think?"

"Oh, wow." I'm quiet for a moment, thinking. I guess I always believed Bev was already doing it. She said Jason really turned her on. She joked about experimenting. Didn't she say that men are like different kinds of food? If you don't try them, how will you know what you like? When I say this she answers, "By now you should know my bark is worse than my bite. I always try ideas out loud just to hear how they sound. Doesn't mean I'll put them in practice. I bet most kids are like that."

"What about Sunny?" I ask. "Have you told her?"

"Sure. And she says what's the big deal? She's been doing it since she was my age."

"So what's stopping you?"

Bev squeezes her hands together anxiously. "It's such a big step. I mean, once you take it there's no going back. The truth is, I'm scared."

"Do you love him?"

Bev shrugs. "Who knows? Sometimes. But sometimes he drives me crazy, he's such a chauvinist. Sometimes I hate myself for acting the helpless dumb blonde just to please him."

"And you're not even a blonde." We both giggle. "What about birth control and all that?"

"He said he'd take care of it." Her lips turn up in a sheepish grin.

"Gee, Bev. I don't know what to say. You're asking the wrong person, considering my experience. And anyway, want the truth? Promise you won't be angry?"

She nods and watches me intently.

"Jason's not good enough for you."

"Maybe not. But I'm no beauty, and I'm too fat and all the girls are crazy for him. I'm lucky to have him. I really want to—sort of. If I *won't*, he'll find someone who *will*."

"Then let him."

"I don't know. All the guys want the same thing. If it's not Jase, it'll be someone else."

"If we all stood together and said no, they'd just have to wait until it's right for both parties. Right? Besides, no one should have the right to your body unless you really want them to. Not just 'sort of.' "

"Right," Bev says without much conviction. She stands up and we start walking again. "I don't know. Maybe I should talk with Sunny again. It seems to have worked out all right for her. Maybe it's just one of those peaks you have to climb before you reach a new plateau. . . . I don't know."

When we finally part, Bev seems just as confused and uncertain as when she first told me about her dilemma. I wish I could have been of more help, but I guess this is something she'll have to think out for herself.

Chapter 10

"Did you see Plunkett today, Mom?" I ask as soon as she gets home with Becky. I'm helping my sister out of her zippered jacket while Mom hangs up her coat. Instead of answering, Mom says, "Turn on Becky's cartoon program, will you, Adri? And then come inside and help me with dinner. Go on inside, Becky. I'll bring you an apple in a minute."

"Apple bapple," Becky says. "Oozy doozy."

"Tickle ickle," I supply, giving her a quick, loving tickle so that she giggles as I set her down in front of the TV and turn on channel 28. And then I hurry back to the kitchen to find out what Mom has to say.

"Let's see, what shall I make for supper?" Mom stands for a moment in the middle of the kitchen, looking uncertain. "I've got a chicken and some ground beef. The beef would be faster, but I better use the chicken before it spoils. Get the rice out of the cabinet for me, will you, a can of V-8 juice, and let's see, a can of chicken bouillon." Mom opens the refrigerator, takes out an armload of things, and goes to the sink. For a few minutes we're both busy getting things together.

"She's really a very caring person," Mom says, referring, I assume, to Martha Plunkett. "Put about a cup of rice on the bottom of the flat casserole, honey, and chop this onion, please." Without a pause she goes on. "It's just as I figured. There's flu going around, and one of the early symptoms is fatigue and irritability. She was really very nice about it. Said she'd make a special effort to see that Becky wasn't overstimulated in the next few days— that perhaps they'd not been sensitive enough to her being 'under the weather.' "

"And what about the nightmare?"

Mom pulls the skin off the chicken breast. "Maybe she was running a low-grade fever, she thought."

"You felt Becky's head Mom! She didn't have a fever."

"Maybe. I don't know. I didn't take her temperature, remember."

"And wetting her pants? Coming home with someone else's underwear?"

Mom's lips pucker. "Adri! I wish you could hear yourself. You sound like you don't believe a word she said. Why should you be so distrustful?" She notices that I'm not doing anything and tells me to distribute the onions over the rice and start the salad. Then she says, "She was really quite obviously contrite. 'I should have sent home a note,' she said. 'When a child wets herself, or soils his or her pants, as they do sometimes at this age, we just change them.' And she showed me a box of clean clothes. jeans, shorts, underwear, T-shirts—and asked me if I saw Becky's pants among them."

"Did you ask why she's so destructive with her toys

96

lately, why she'd scribble those awful pictures in my book?"

"I did. And she reminded me that I must have forgotten how you were at that age. In fact, I was embarrassed. She pulled out one of her child-rearing books and immediately turned to a page which described the three-and-a-half-year-old . . . as a child who feels added tensions and often expresses these feelings in many ways: stuttering, eye blinking, thumb sucking, nose picking, even—masturbating." Mom smiles quickly at me. "At least she's not doing *that.*"

I absorb this information for a while, as I begin to wash the salad greens for dinner, and then ask, "And what about the kissing with the tongue in the mouth?"

"Adri, stop it. Enough. There's nothing wrong with Becky. Everything that's happening is perfectly normal for this age. Now stop it. You're beginning to get me angry."

I can't stop it. I have to know everything. "But just answer that one question. What did she say about the tongue business?"

Mom sighs, a long-suffering, irritated sigh. "I didn't ask. It was just too insulting, and I'd already gone on like an interrogator for far too long. I just didn't ask. Now, let's not have another word about it."

Is it all normal, I wonder, as I open the cans and Mom places the chicken pieces over the rice. Am I making a big drama out of a whole lot of little happenings that are just typical three-and-a-half-year-old behavior? Did I hate preschool so much that I interpret everything that happens to Becky from that perspective?

"I'm going in to be with Becky," I say as soon as I've finished fixing the salad. For some reason I'm really angry at my mother. I just don't believe a word of what Plunkett said. Something's going on at that preschool that's not right. I just know it. I knew it at Becky's age. I tried to tell Mom and she wouldn't listen. And now Becky's trying to tell also, and no one's listening. I don't know what it is that's going on, but one way or another I'm going to find out.

When the phone rings later that evening and Dad says it's Ryan, an alarm clock goes off in my body. I pick up the phone as if it might explode.

"Adrienne, it's me, Ryan," he says.

"I know. Dad said. Hi."

"Listen. Let's talk. If I came by in a few minutes could you come out?"

"Yes." An enormous jolt of joy zaps through me.

"Good. See you soon."

He hangs up, leaving me breathless, and then I begin to wonder what it is he wants to talk about. I hurry to my room to check my hair and change to my new, white sweater, and almost before I'm changed the bell rings. "I'll get it," I call, running down the hall. I stick my head into the living room and say, "I'm just going out for a little while. That's Ryan."

"Have fun," Dad calls, and Mom smiles.

"Let's walk," Ryan says at the door. "It's so nice tonight."

He doesn't take my hand. We walk apart, although he does touch my back lightly when we cross a street.

"I thought about what you said today, about Becky, and figured maybe you'd want to talk about it."

"Oh!" I let out my breath, not realizing until then that I was holding it. He wants to be my *friend!* My heart sings.

"You said it's a long story. What's wrong? Is there anything I can do to help?"

"I don't know. I don't even know for sure that anything is wrong, but let me tell you what's happening and you decide."

I tell him about all the changes in Becky in recent months, from the happy pictures on the fridge to the dark ugly scribbles in my book, from calm and playful to overtired, irritable, and scared. I tell him, also, about Mom's conversation with Martha Plunkett and how she persuaded Mom that everything's normal. "And she didn't ask about the way she kissed you that night at the house," I add, able to say it only because we're walking at night and it's dark.

"She kissed me that way once before—the night we went to the Christmas party. Remember? I told you I thought she was precocious and you took it to mean 'smart.' " His voice drops lower. "And there's something else you don't know. That same evening, before you came in, I offered to play hide-and-seek with her."

"So?"

99

"Before I could say who'd be it, she did a funny thing." He pauses. "She started to undress."

"What?" I turn to Ryan, stopping in the street, incredulous. *"What?"*

"I was just as surprised, and I said, 'Becky, *what are you doing?'* "

"What did she say?"

"She seemed confused and backed off, and when I asked her again she said, 'That's what you do in hide-and-seek.' "

I am too dumbfounded to ask what happened next, but Ryan says, "I just changed the subject and sat her down to look at pictures in a magazine. And then you and your mother came in."

"What's going on with her!" I cry.

Ryan puts a hand on my shoulder as we walk along Vista del Valle. A dog barks as we pass his territory. A night jogger huffs past us, nodding greeting. When we reach the little park near the highway, Ryan takes the path that leads to the flagpole, where there's a low brick wall we can sit on. I decide now to tell him everything . . . about my discomfort with Martha Plunkett at the party, about my weird flashbacks to scenes that have no meaning to me, or that I have no memory of, about this phrase that goes through my head so often about the rabbits.

"In some way I think it's all connected . . . these flashbacks or memories . . . and maybe they are memories . . . and what is or isn't happening now to Becky."

Ryan listens intently, never taking his eyes from my

face. I realize before even beginning my story that I run the risk of his thinking me batty. But in all the time I've known him he's never made fun of anything anyone said, no matter how off the wall.

"It's such a respectable school," Ryan muses. "Plunkett's been in business for ages. My God. She doesn't smoke. She's a regular churchgoer. She's . . . a pillar of the community. I think she's got kids there now who are the children of some of her first students."

"I know."

"And it just doesn't seem possible something like this . . . sexual abuse . . ."

"Sexual abuse?"

"Yes. Don't you hear what you've been saying? Maybe that's why you can't get close."

"You mean . . . why I'm so . . . *frigid.*"

"I mean, why you don't feel comfortable about closeness." He takes my cold hands in his. "As I was saying, it just doesn't seem possible that something like sexual abuse could go on this long without someone being onto it. Surely, parents would notice . . ."

"Or some of the other teachers would tell. Except"—I hesitate, thinking—"they've got the same teachers now as when I was there."

"So it could be a conspiracy . . . against the children."

"It's too bizarre. Isn't it?"

Ryan stares at me for a time, then says, "Yes. But it's possible."

101

"Oh, my God! Then how can I find out if it's true? And what can I do to stop them from hurting Becky!"

"And the other children maybe . . . probably . . ."

"What should I *do?*"

"*We* do. I'd like to help. It's pretty rotten if anything *is* really going on."

"I'm going to ask Becky. Just point blank ask her!"

"I doubt she'd tell. She's probably been warned or maybe even threatened."

"Threatened? Yes. You're probably right. Then what can I do?"

"For now I think the only thing you can do is spend a lot of time with her. Watch and listen. Get more evidence. And try to dig into your own memories and see what you come up with."

And so, that's how we leave it. Walking back to the house there's a new bond between us of mutual concern. Ryan makes no advances, so I guess he's transferred his feelings to the blonde, and though it hurts me to know he wants someone else, it's also a relief not to have to deal with it, especially now.

For the next two weeks Becky seems her old normal self. She apparently kicked the virus Plunkett thought she might be coming down with—if, indeed, she actually had it. And she comes home from school with bright, finger-painted sheets, looped-paper necklaces, a Styrofoam cup planted with a bean seed she is to water regularly.

Each evening I offer to bathe and put her to bed. I use

the time to talk with her and ask questions. "What did you do in school today? Tell me a story. How is Peter Rabbit?"

And I get silly, giggly answers—like, "Little girl went to school. She rides a horse. She rides a elephant. She rides a giant." (Giggle, giggle—watching me to see if I realize it's funny.) "Then she buyed a rabbit. Then she dyed the rabbit. Then she . . ."

"Died the rabbit? You mean killed the rabbit, Becky?"

"No! No! She make the rabbit blue, then green. Then she . . ." and on and on with a singsong story that as far as I can see is little more than a catalog of "things."

It isn't until later that I realize she is actually pronouncing her *r*'s now. Delighted, I give her a big hug.

During one such happy time together, while she's playing with her hand puppets, I say, "Becky, honey. Is there anything about Treehouse that you don't like? Anything you want to tell me?"

Without answering, she suddenly smashes the lady puppet on her right hand viciously against the Pinocchio puppet on her left, growling, "Bad, bad, bad boy!"

And I don't know if she's just completing the story she started earlier about Pinocchio and his mother, or if, in her own way, she is answering me.

"Anything new?" Ryan asks each day, and I have to say no. Not only have the flashbacks stopped for me, but Becky is behaving like a perfectly normal three-and-a-half-year-old.

"Maybe I *have* made too much of all this," I say to him

at school one day when he stops at my French class to ask.

"Maybe. But maybe Plunkett got scared when your Mom got so inquisitive and cooled whatever's going on."

"Ryan?" Susan calls from four doors down the hall.

"Coming!" he calls back. And to me he says, "She needs to check a math problem."

"It's okay. I understand. Go ahead. If anything happens, I'll let you know."

I turn my back and go into French, not wanting to see Ryan join his girlfriend. It hurts knowing he's close to someone else.

Life seems to be in a holding pattern. Bev's stalling Jason. Becky's thriving. Hollow though my social life is, at least I'm not having nightmares.

And then, two weeks later, it starts again.

Chapter 11

"Her rabbit died," Mom says quietly when she comes home one afternoon, warning me with a stern look not to ask questions. Becky's eyes are red and her pale face is streaked with dirt. She must have cried all the way home in the car. Mom takes her directly into the bedroom. She washes her face, puts her to bed, and sits by her side singing lullabies until she falls asleep. Mom leaves the bedroom door slightly ajar and puts a finger to her lips as we walk back to the kitchen. Only there does she tell the story.

"Martha Plunkett took me aside when I came for Becky and told me what happened and that Becky was very upset. She explained that one of the boys took her rabbit out of its cage and the rabbit bit him. The child got angry, grabbed it by the ears, and threw it against the wall. Of course the animal died."

"And Becky *saw* this?"

"So it seems."

"How terrible! How absolutely awful! Why do they bring rabbits into preschool if children are too young to handle them?"

"I asked that too. She said it's important to teach children how to care for and be gentle with animals—and that most of the time they are. There are, of course, rare exceptions."

"Rare! My rabbit died too. Remember?"

"I do, and that's why I'm especially concerned. It does seem an odd coincidence. And yet . . ."

"What?"

"Plunkett was so concerned, so gentle with Becky. She crouched down to look her directly in the eyes and in the kindest, most sympathetic voice said how very sorry she was that it happened and that, no matter what, they all loved her."

"*No matter what*—they all loved her? What does that mean?"

Mom, who has been sitting on a kitchen chair facing me, rises now and slowly unbuttons her jacket. "Now, don't start that again. People aren't always as precise as you. She was just being nice. Don't start reading all kinds of meanings into it!"

The subject is closed. I wonder if Mom has always buried her head in the sand or if she doesn't want to see what might be happening because it's too horrible to contemplate. I used to think I was lucky having a mother who worked. She's too busy to want to know every move I make, not that I do anything wrong. Some kids have moms with nothing else to do but keep an eye on them. They can't make a move without their moms putting their two cents in. Right now I'd give anything for a mother like that. It seems to me that Mom doesn't pay enough attention.

When Dad gets the story later, the part about what Plunkett said to Becky is left out. He, also, doesn't see anything unusual and says, "It's too bad she had to see the animal die like that, but death is part of life, too, and this is a way for her to come to deal with it."

And so that evening I write in my journal, "It's up to me. If something like child abuse is happening at Treehouse, I'm going to find out. I wonder if Ryan would help?"

I present the idea to Ryan the next day. This time I get to his geometry classroom early to catch him before he goes in. The blond girl, Susan, sees me and stops to chat. She tells me what a great brain Ryan is in math and asks if I'm waiting for him. "We have a quiz today," she informs me, suggesting, I suppose, that he has no time to talk.

When Ryan appears, he seems surprised and embarrassed, not knowing which of us to look at. Susan smiles radiantly at him and I feel like walking off. I wish she'd just leave me alone with him for two minutes. I'm not trying to take him away from her.

"Is anything wrong?" Ryan asks of me.

"Ryan, the bell's going to ring in a minute and we have that quiz," Susan says.

"I know! Be back in a minute," he answers, and takes my arm to walk me down the hall to French.

In the minute we have I explain my plan to him, that I

want to pick up Becky early tomorrow and look around the school a little. Would he like to come along?

"I've got swim practice," he says, disappointed.

"Oh. . . . Oh, that's all right. I can go alone!"

"No . . . that's okay. I'll make some excuse. We'll go right after last period. Meet you outside—at the usual place."

I'm so relieved I want to laugh and cry. The bell rings. Ryan turns and runs back down the hall. "Good luck on the quiz," I call after him.

It's easy to arrange with Mom. She even likes the idea of my picking Becky up early and maybe taking her to the zoo for a special outing. "It's just what she needs right now," she says. "I'll tell Plunkett in the morning that you're coming."

"Oh, no, Mom, please don't! I'm not sure yet just when I'll get there, and they may keep Becky in the office waiting for who knows how long." That's the reason I give Mom, surprised at how easily the lie comes out. The truth is, of course, that it would spoil everything if Plunkett knew I was coming.

"Adri, dear, they have rules. It disturbs the school routine." And she tells me how parents are dissuaded from dropping by without notice, which seems strange to me.

Somehow I persuade her, reasoning that all the structured activities take place in the morning and that the children who remain all day are pretty much free to rest or play at whatever they like.

And so the next day Ryan and I meet right after school and take the bus that goes near the preschool.

"I've been thinking a lot about it," I tell him on the ride. "We're going to have to pretend we don't know the rules, because if we stop at the office they'll just keep us there until they bring Becky—and we won't see a thing."

"Which means we'll have to wander into the backyard and see what we can while we can."

"What should we be looking for? I mean, if there really is any abuse going on—well, do we listen for screams, or peer into classrooms, or what?"

"I don't know. I have a feeling we'll know when we see it. Cameras and lighting equipment, maybe, to make kid porno films. A teacher alone with a kid doing what he— or she?—shouldn't. I don't really know."

Cameras and lighting equipment. The words stir an old image. Was it the *sun* burning my eyes or *bright lights* as I stood painting at the easel, feeling cold. Was I undressed under the apron? Being photographed? The thought brings a frightened shudder and Ryan asks what's wrong. I shake my head, not able to say because it's too bizarre; it can't have really happened. And now I can hardly wait to get to the school. I swear, if I find anything happening like that to Becky I'll kill the woman! I'll just beat her until she's blood and guts!

When we reach the house I'm so nervous I can't talk. As we turn into the walk, Ryan raises his eyebrows in an anxious way he has and says, "Well, this is it." We cut across the lawn to the driveway, which leads to a six-foot picket fence and a door with no door pull. Ryan stands on a rock, reaches over the fence, searches around, and finds the latch. The door squeaks noisily on its hinge and we freeze for an instant expecting to be discovered. When no one comes, we enter the yard behind the house, closing the door.

It's a typical nursery school playground. Against one side of the fence there's a nice elm, which shades a long wooden bench. Another tree nearby has a seat encircling it. Ahead is a sandbox studded with pails and trucks. Painting easels are lined up side by side in rows. On the lawn are a jungle gym, a slide, tires hanging from a tree, wagons, and tricycles.

The school buildings form three sides to the yard. Except for a single child lying across a swing on his stomach watching us, there is no one in view.

I peer into a room of the main house, but a curtain obscures the view. From somewhere inside a typewriter clacks steadily. Maybe this is the office building and the classrooms are in the other houses. As we advance across the lawn the child jumps off the swing and goes running into the building to our right, "Mrs. T, Mrs. T!" he cries. "Someone's here!"

"Oh, boy. That's it!" Ryan exclaims. "Smile. Here they come."

Mrs. T. emerges almost at once with the little boy at her heels. She turns, says something to someone in the room, then in a stern voice calls out, "What are you two doing here? How did you get in?"

"Hi, Mrs. T," I say. "I'm Becky's sister Adrienne. You

know me. And this is my friend Ryan. Didn't Mom tell you I'd be coming by early to pick Becky up?"

She looks behind us, which makes me turn around to see what it is she's seeing. Mrs. Plunkett closes a door and strides across the grass to us.

"That's all right, Dorothy. I'll handle it." She nods toward the building Mrs. T came out of, and I don't know if I read a warning in her eyes or if I'm dramatizing. Then in a friendly tone she says, "Oh, it's you Adrienne, and Ryan, isn't it? Don't you know you're supposed to come through the office?"

"We didn't want to bother you, Mrs. Plunkett. We thought it might be fun to surprise Becky. We're picking her up early to take her to the zoo," Ryan says.

"Well, just come back with me and wait in the office. Becky's resting now. When rest time is over, one of the aides will bring her out."

If we go into the office, the whole trip will have been pointless. A wave of disappointment flushes over me, and then I say, "Mrs. Plunkett—I wonder if we could look around the school a little. It's such a pretty setting, and I've thought maybe I'd like to be a nursery school teacher some day. Couldn't we?" I plead.

She hesitates. "I'm really very busy."

"That's okay. We'll just poke around by ourselves. We won't disturb anything," Ryan says.

"No. That's not possible," Plunkett replies. "I suppose I can spare a *few* minutes. Come along."

Ryan gives me a surprised glance and takes my hand. We follow Mrs. Plunkett back to the main building. Her

111

necklace clicks against her chest as she hurries along. A slightly sour smell mixed with perfume reaches my nostrils and I want to draw back, pull away. There is a memory . . . that same smell . . . someone—Plunkett?—pulling me along a dim hallway toward . . .

"This is the main building, where we fix snacks and conduct our business, and where I live," Plunkett says in a perfunctory tone. She takes a clump of keys from a board and says, "I'll show you the classrooms."

She unlocks a door to one of the buildings and takes us through the rooms. Colorful posters brighten the walls. There are red and yellow tables and chairs, and bookshelves full of bright toys—airplanes, boxes of blocks, dolls. There are models of fire trucks and rocket ships to climb in and on. There's a corner for playing house with a child-sized kitchen and play dishes, pots, and pans. Pails identified with children's names line a long wall; there are paintings or hand-made objects tucked into some of them.

"It's really nice," Ryan says. "Makes me wish I went to preschool."

"Yes," Mrs. Plunkett says. "We do our best. Let's move on now. The children who stay after lunch will be in the next building. They're all taking naps, so we'll just peek in the window." She marches along, opening the door to the outside and holding it for us. I hear a sound, voices, a child crying. In one swift movement Ryan turns and strides across the room in the direction of the voices, and is gone.

"Ryan!" Mrs. Plunkett calls. With the speed of a much

112

younger person, she runs after him. I follow. We find Ryan down a hall in front of a bathroom, its door ajar. Inside are a male teacher and a little boy, the child bare below the waist and crying.

"Bobby had an accident," the male teacher says, smiling up at us. "He's kind of embarrassed."

"Please!" Mrs. Plunkett says. "This is exactly why I don't like visitors to come unannounced. Children are very sensitive to strangers. Please! Come along, now!"

I question Ryan with my eyes, wondering if he saw anything more than what I did. His face is blank.

I will never know what is in the third building, the building with the very large room in which perhaps twenty or so children are resting, because we are not invited into it. But through the window I can see them. They are lying on mats, little girls and boys, some smaller than Becky, some bigger, some curled up in fetal positions sucking their thumbs, some resting on their stomachs or backs, holding blankets. Mrs. T sits on a stool, watching. Behind her, on a shelf, are cages with rabbits and hamsters and turtles. Mrs. T puts her finger to her lips and smiles back at us. It all looks just as Mom says—a beautifully equipped and well-run school, with nothing—nothing that I can see—amiss.

When we return to the office, Mrs. Plunkett offers us some coffee and asks after Ryan's mother and family. Then she excuses herself to go get Becky. In the brief silence before her return I ask Ryan what he saw.

"He was bent over the kid's bottom. The kid seemed

113

to be in pain, or scared, or both. I don't know. But his explanation made sense. I really don't know."

We sit waiting, both silent and thinking, and I'm sure something's odd, but I can't think what. I hear Plunkett returning, and Becky's voice, high with excitement. And suddenly I remember the little boy on the swing, outside, watching. That's it! Why would he be *outside* when all the other children are inside?

And I am three again, holding tight to my high perch atop the jungle gym with instructions to stay put and keep watch and if anyone comes . . . It's a game, you see, though I don't find it much fun. I want to come down because it hurts holding on so long. But Plunkett is the Law, and the Law says that Adri is the lookout, and until she's told otherwise . . . that's where she stays.

Chapter 12

There is no time to dig deeper into these thoughts because Becky arrives rubbing her eyes from sleep but full of delight at this unexpected outing. Plunkett pats her head and tells us to have a good time as she shows us out the door.

On our way to the zoo Ryan and I are unable to talk about the last half hour because of Becky, but we're both distracted in our own ways. When our eyes meet, Ryan's are full of questions. And keeping up small talk is especially hard because my head whirls with thoughts it wants to explore.

Finally we are at the children's petting zoo. We release Becky's hands, and she goes flying off to the puppy pit. She sits among a half dozen lovable dogs, touching, cuddling, scrabbling after them on her knees.

We stand at the railing, looking down. "It's coming back, Ryan," I say, almost in a whisper. "I'm beginning to make sense of all those strange dreams." I look up at him, trembling with excitement. It's such a fragile thing, these wisps of memory, so incomplete, so intense, so real and yet unreal. And this is hardly the place to explore it, here in the bright sun with children running around and desert tortoises underfoot and peacocks spreading their feathers and crying their strange mating cries.

"You know how I told you once that I hardly remember anything before I was five or six? Well, maybe the reason is that I don't want to remember."

A young mother wheels a stroller into place beside us and points to the puppies. "Doggie," she says to the child. Then, seeing us, she smiles. I smile back politely but edge away.

"I think things happened to me at Treehouse," I whisper. "The boy we saw—he was probably a lookout. Watching for unexpected visitors, while inside, maybe they were doing things to the kids."

"What things?" Ryan whispers back, glancing toward the young mother and moving still farther away around the circular railing.

"Playing games . . . hide-and-seek, for example. The kids were always told to hide, and the Treehouse teachers would always find them."

Ryan stares at me, waiting, and I look away. "The kids were always naked. . . . And the teachers did things."

"What things?" His face reddens.

My mouth is very dry and I open it to speak, but the words don't come out. "I can't. I think you know."

"Adri! Ryan! Look at me!" Becky calls from the pit. A brown and white puppy with floppy ears is licking her face.

"That's wonderful!" I call. My hands cramp from the

116

tight grip I have been keeping on the railing. I am sure now that I was violated. I remember trying to get away, running, being caught. A sharp pain sears my private place. I jam my fist against my mouth to stifle the need to scream.

"Let's go," Ryan says. "You've got to tell your parents. They've got to know so they can do something about it."

A tear wets my cheek and I shake my head. "They'd never believe it. They'd wonder why I didn't say anything years ago. They'd say I have a vivid imagination and that maybe I dreamed it, because if it was really true, how come none of the other kids have said anything all these years?"

"You've got to tell them. Otherwise, if it's happening now, it will keep on happening."

Becky climbs out of the pit, all smiles. I take her hand and walk across the dusty ground to the next exhibit. Rabbits.

It's probably the most popular exhibit in the petting zoo. A teenage volunteer decides which children get to hold a rabbit and for how long. "They get very nervous," she explains to us when we arrive. "Too much handling."

"Do you want to hold a rabbit?" I ask Becky who stands watching solemnly, thumb in mouth.

"They look so soft and cuddly," Ryan says. "How about it, Becky?"

The girl volunteer picks up a rabbit and offers it. But Becky buries her face against my hip and cries, "No!"

Ryan takes the animal and holds it gently, stroking its white, white fur. "She's probably scared, after what happened to her own rabbit. Maybe if *you* hold it she'll see that it's okay." He plants the rabbit in my arms before I can respond and I close my eyes, remembering—the feel of it, the smell, the softness against my cheek, the heartbeat fluttering rapidly under my fingertips, the warmth.

I'll let you hold the rabbit . . . if . . .

. . . if you do as I say . . .

. . . if you touch Randy where I tell you . . .

. . . if you don't try to run away when we play doctor . . .

. . . if you smile when these good people make nice to you . . .

. . . and if you tell anyone *. . . because it's our own special secret . . . then this is what we'll do to Rabbit!*

"Oh!"

Stricken, I push the rabbit back into the attendant's hands and rush away. I am shaking and wet with a cold sweat. I cover my face with my hands and try to make myself as small a target as possible.

"Adri! What's wrong?" Ryan asks, coming after me. He turns me around, then puts his arms around me.

"It's okay, it's okay," he croons. "Whatever it was, it's over. It's okay . . ."

But it isn't. The shivering goes on for a long while, and when the cold finally passes and I can walk, the zoo volunteer comes up to ask if I'm okay. Does Ryan want to take me to the infirmary?

"It's nothing, thanks," I explain, embarrassed at how many people are watching. "I was just . . . I'm getting over the flu." I turn to Becky, who is holding on to Ryan's shirt. "Let's go, guys. Okay?"

Becky, sobered by what she doesn't understand, accepts my hand and Ryan's without a word of protest. And we head home.

"Adri . . . just a second. We have to talk," Ryan says when we get to the door and Becky has gone into the house.

I hesitate, then turn to him. "I know what you're going to say. But even if I told them, even if they believed it all —and it's so crazy, who would believe it? But even if they did . . . what could they do? We have no evidence."

My words stop Ryan for an instant, but then he says, "They could talk to other parents, ask if they noticed anything funny."

"Sure. Can you imagine them phoning one of the other parents, or calling a meeting of parents and saying 'I think my daughter is being abused at the preschool. My older daughter says she thinks it happened to her.' They'd never be able to look any of those people in the eye again!"

"You've got to tell them, Adri. Even so. You have to. Maybe they wouldn't listen when you were little, but they have to listen now. They have to!"

"Why? Adults don't have to do anything. They have all the power. Children are supposed to be seen and not heard; be nice to the man; kiss Auntie; do what Mommy says. Don't you know that?"

"Adri . . ." he tries again, but he's run out of arguments. "Oh, Adri."

"Right," I say. "Thanks for coming along, and thanks for listening, and thanks for believing me." And then I turn abruptly and go into the house.

I am obsessed with my new knowledge. As if I have a scab I pick at it and pull at it and soon it's oozing memories. The next days go by and I am completely tuned in to myself. It all comes rushing back—the drive to a farm where there is a barn with stadium seats and people watching while all of us children—boys and girls—nude —do things to each other and have things done to us by grown-ups. The threat of harm to our mothers and fathers if we tell.

I can't believe what goes through my head. It has to have happened, or else I am really mad. But if it happened, how could it have gone unnoticed by parents? And worse, how could any human being do such things to a child?

"Speak to your father, if you can't talk to your mom," Bev says gently. "Maybe you need some psychological help."

"You don't believe me," I say, a statement of fact.

"Of course I do! That's why I think you need help."

She doesn't believe me. She can't, just as *they* wouldn't be able to believe anything so bizarre.

I feel trapped, because if it really happened, then Becky is in danger. Some things must have already happened. But how far have they gone? I have to have *evidence*—but how can I get it? How?

Ryan has begun to walk me from class to class again. He makes no effort to touch me. I think he does it out of a sense of pity. I don't much care what his reasons are, because I'm so absorbed with fear and rage and worry that I think of little else.

"Tell them," he urges again and again. And finally, "If you don't, I will."

So one night a few days later, when Becky is in bed, I tell Mom and Dad that I have to talk with them. And I tell them what I think happened to me when I was little.

"Darling," Mom says, taking both my hands in hers. The expression on her face is full of compassion and love, but I am wary. Mom is so good at denial. She exchanges a look with Dad that says "Humor her."

"These nightmares must be horrible. But it can't be *true*. You loved preschool. Why have you focused on Martha Plunkett? Did she spank you when you were little and have you built this elaborate fantasy through the years to get back at her?"

I feel the sob start deep inside my chest and put my hands over my mouth to stifle it. No wonder I have never trusted Mom, never could feel close.

"Could it be possible?" Dad asks. "Helen? Adrienne is not the kind of child to make up such stories."

"Of course not. How could such things have happened and we not know about it?"

"You said yourself I changed!" I cry. "You said I was such an open, loving kid when I started at the school and later I became so secretive and remote. You said that!"

"Yes, I did, but between one and five years of age personalities are forming. You just grew into the kind of person you would be."

"What's the use? Anything I say you won't believe.

You never did! Forget it." I get up to leave the room. "I didn't want to tell you. Ryan insisted!" I throw back over my shoulder.

"Ryan! He knows? How could you?" Mom cries.

"That's all you care about, appearances!" I cry, running out of the room. It's too much for her, the truth, but at least she can vent her fear by blaming me for telling Ryan.

I hear them talking together for a long while, and finally Daddy comes to my room. "It's a terrible accusation you're making, Adrienne. It's too awful to contemplate, much less believe and accept. We think you should see someone—a therapist—someone you can talk out your anger with."

"You think I'm crazy, don't you?"

"No, I don't. But I do think you've carried a whole lot of hostility against your mother—and against this Plunkett woman—for a very long time, and you should try to find out why."

"Go away," I say, turning my head into the pillow. "Go away. Nobody can make me believe it's all in my head!"

Chapter 13

Mom sets up an appointment for me to see a Dr. Shapiro, but I don't want to go.

Bev says she thinks it's a good idea. "At least you can talk about how you feel about sex."

Ryan thinks it's a good idea too. "If you get it all out in the open, maybe she can tell you how much, if any of it, is fantasy. Maybe you've created this horrible fantasy to avoid getting close."

Nobody really believes it happened. Not even Ryan.

And then one day I overhear Mom tell Dad that she's taking Becky to the doctor the next day. Becky has a peculiar rash in her groin.

"A *rash?*" Dad asks, suddenly on the alert. "Where? Let me see."

They go into Becky's room and I slip down the hall to watch.

"Hi, ducky lucky," Dad greets with false gaiety. "Mommy says something hurts you. Want to show Daddy where?"

From the doorway I see Dad bend over Becky. He

straightens up and says, "That's peculiar. It looks pretty inflamed. What do you suppose it is?"

Mom shrugs. "I don't know. Maybe she sat in the sandbox and wet herself and the sand irritated her there."

"Do you remember anything like this ever happening to Adrienne?"

"Now, Mark. I know what you're thinking. Adri's got us all coming and going with those stories!"

Dad turns back to Becky. "What happened, sweetie? Did you hurt yourself? Did you play in the sandbox today? Did anyone hurt you there?"

I creep closer to Becky's bed so I can see her when she answers. She is staring up at Daddy with those big, innocent brown eyes, but they have a distant, dull look to them. When Daddy repeats his question, she shakes her head.

"Well, I don't know what to think," Dad says. "Maybe you should put a little ointment on it to take down the inflammation. And I think you *should* take her to the doctor tomorrow. Call me when you get through."

My heart leaps. It's happened to Becky too. Poor baby. Poor baby.

When my parents leave the room I go back in, gather her up in my arms, and cuddle her. "Becky, sweet Becky," I sing. "I won't let them hurt you any more! Tomorrow, for sure, the doctor will tell Mom and Dad . . . and then they'll have to believe me!"

Mom takes the day off to take Becky to the doctor, but already by morning some of the redness is gone. I go to school but can hardly wait to get home to find out what happened.

When I come into the kitchen, Mom's cleaning out the can cupboard and humming. Becky is playing with her dolls in the bedroom.

"The doctor?" Mom asks, as if she has forgotten already. "Oh, yes. He just said to bathe her with a solution of Epsom salts and then put a little Vaseline over the rash."

"But what caused it?" I persist.

"Nylon panties. He says he sees it very often. Children perspire or wet themselves and the nylon retains the moisture and rubs the skin. He suggests I get some cotton underwear."

"Is that all?" I ask.

"Of course. Why? Did you think it might be something else?"

"Yes, I think it could be something else!"

"Don't be fresh with me, young lady! And stop this vendetta against Treehouse. You have a very fertile imagination. Use it in your writing. There is *nothing* going on at Treehouse—nothing that hasn't a perfectly logical explanation."

Mom and I stare each other down. I'm the first to turn away. There's only one way to prove what's happening, and that's to get it out of Becky. And if what I believe is true, Becky has been warned that terrible things will happen to Mom, to Dad, even to me if she says anything. That's why Peter Rabbit died. She wasn't killed by any child in the school. No. I don't believe that for a minute.

Peter Rabbit was killed by *Plunkett*—or one of the other teachers—killed to show what would happen to others Becky loves if she tells a single living soul.

I am very nervous. It's after dinner two days later and Dad, Becky, and I are doing dishes because Mom's gone for an open house at her school tonight. Dad makes jokes about his harem—Becky and Mom and me—but I can't join in the lightheartedness. Every time I look at Becky—who is drying the pots—I get a twinge of fear.

"I'll get Becky ready for bed," I tell Dad later, dreading the next half hour.

"Thanks, honey. I'll be in in a little while to say goodnight." He goes into the living room to read the evening paper.

"Let's go, Beck," I say, taking my little sister's hand. I have set it all up. Ryan helped me plan how to do it. I don't know if it will work, but we'll see. I hope the tape recorder doesn't make any noise to distract her.

"Tonight we're going to play games before bed," I tell her, "right after your bath."

"What games?" Becky asks, looking up at me with those trusting, innocent eyes.

"Doll games. You'll see. But first, into the tub."

I am very careful washing around her private parts, because she cries out when the cloth touches her there. I bite my lip to keep still, because I know how it must feel. And I don't want to let my thoughts range over the first time it happened for me. Or the times after.

When she is bathed and dressed in her yellow and

126

white pajamas with the white slippers ending in little pompoms at the toes, she looks as fresh and beautiful as a daisy. Heart pounding, I lead her into the bedroom, where I've set out a box of hand puppets and dolls on the white shag rug. Passing the tape recorder, I flip on the switch. Becky doesn't notice as she drops down on the rug and starts to explore the box of toys.

I sit opposite her, legs crossed, and take out a brown-bear hand puppet first. I put it on my right hand and say, in a high-pitched pretend voice, "Let's play a game, okay, Becky? What shall we play?"

"Teapot!" she exclaims eagerly.

"Wonderful," I say in my high-pitched voice. "What do we do?"

Becky jumps to her feet and starts to enact "I'm a little teapot." She bends down to show how short and stout she is, and points out one arm to show her spout, then bends to the side as she pretends to pour herself out.

Brown Bear claps his hands and says, "That's very good, Becky-wecky. And what else do you play?"

Becky drops down to the rug again and picks up a doll, examining it closely, looking under its dress, and pulling off its tiny pants. "TV star."

"TV star!" My pulse jumps. Yes, that's what we played when I was in preschool! But how can I get her to describe it? "Show me how you play," I say in the high-pitched bear voice.

Suddenly on guard, Becky becomes stiff and watchful.

I pretend not to notice; instead I speak through the puppet. "Brown Bear *never* tells anyone's secrets. That's

127

because I'm just a puppet, and my mouth doesn't really open. See? It's sewn shut!" I hold the puppet close to Becky's face. She examines it for a long moment while I hold my breath, not wanting to make any more sounds than I have to. I wait. Her eyes still on Brown Bear, she says softly, "I can't tell."

"Why?"

She hesitates and gazes down at her hands. "I'm scared."

"Of me? Of telling Brown Bear?"

Becky nods. I ask who made her promise.

Again she hesitates. I can see her struggling to decide if it's okay to answer at least that question. Finally she says, "Mrs. Plunkett. And Harry too. They said Mommy wouldn't love me if I told."

I close my eyes for a moment and take a deep breath. In a voice too near my own I say, "That's not true, Becky! Mommy will always love you. Honest. Cross my heart!" I move the puppet arms in a cross over its chest. "Anyway, I already know."

"You do?" Becky's eyes open wide. She seems relieved her secret isn't so secret after all.

Brown Bear nods solemnly. "But tell me anyway." I use the bear to push the box of toys closer to Becky. "And show me."

For the next few minutes she sorts through the toys, taking some out, putting some back. It's taking so long that I'm beginning to think she may have forgotten my question. But she hasn't. She places three dolls on the outside of a circle of other dolls and little toy animals.

128

"Who are they?" Brown Bear asks in his special voice, pointing to the three outside the circle.

"That's the director . . . and that's the other director. And over here are the lights. And this is the lady with the camera."

"But who *are* they?"

"Mrs. T . . . and Mrs. Plunkett, and Harry."

"And now what happens?" My mouth is dry and my eyes burn from watching Becky without once blinking.

As if in a trance she starts to reenact the TV-star game. Very clearly, in a singsong voice, she explains that the children, without clothes on, march around the circle to music played on the record player. Then, when the music stops, a girl and a boy go to the center of the circle. The camera moves closer. At this point, she stops and looks directly into my eyes, suddenly aware of what she is doing.

"Go on, Becky," I say in my normal voice, in such a way as not to intimidate her. "It's okay. Some secrets are not meant to be kept. You can tell Adri and Brown Bear. Nothing bad will happen. I promise!"

Hesitantly she picks up a girl doll and a boy doll and shows the boy doll putting his hand where it has no right to be on the girl doll's body. A moment later she holds the boy doll's body close to the girl doll's mouth and explains what the girl is supposed to do. She watches me for reaction, and I strain to keep my face expressionless. Besides, it's not unexpected. It's a scene that has played in my mind many times in the last few weeks. I am past the stage of repulsion.

But Daddy isn't. I glance up, suddenly aware that he is standing in the doorway. Becky's back is to him. The look on his face is one of shock and horror. I give him the slightest of nods to stop him from intruding and go on with my questions.

"How do you play hide-and-seek?"

"How did Peter Rabbit really die?"

"When you were tied to the chair, what did the grown-ups do? Did it hurt?"

Using dolls and pencils, she demonstrates and describes horrendous acts. Things she was made to do or were done to her by adults, female as well as male. I listen without judging, for who am I to judge. I am cold and sick with knowing, even though I knew the answers long before I asked the questions.

When the last question is answered, Brown Bear kisses Becky. "You're a very good girl to share your secrets with me," he says in a voice that is breaking. Becky's face blooms into a joyous smile.

When I glance up to the doorway, Daddy is leaning against the frame. One arm shields his eyes and his body is shaking with silent sobs.

Chapter 14

It's as if Pandora's box has been unlocked and all the evil has flown out. I feel good, free, normal. Becky's secrets are also mine, and to have them given words proves my instincts were true.

"Good-night, sweet Becky," I say, as I help her climb into bed and cover her. Her arms reach out to me and I hold her for a long moment, feeling especially close, conscious that my tears are wetting her hair.

"Brown Bear," she says, as she lies down again. And I bring the puppet to the bed and lay it on the pillow beside her. She turns to face it, a serious expression on her face, and I wonder what she's thinking.

Dad comes in, clearing his throat. His eyes are red. Gazing down at Becky, he has the most sorrowful and tender look. He clears his throat again and says, with enormous control, "Good-night, sweetheart. Happy dreams," then bends to kiss her quickly on the forehead.

I click off the tape recorder and carry it out of the room, following Dad. He waits for me in the hall and puts an arm around my shoulder, whispering, "Adri. I'm so sorry."

By the time we reach the living room, his pity has changed to rage. "I don't know if I should phone the police right now or go get that Plunkett woman and string her up!" He paces back and forth. "How could we have let this happen?"

I'm exhausted. I drop into a chair and put my head back, eyes closed.

"My God! All these years it's been going on. All those innocent little children! Those perverts! Those disgusting perverts! Jail isn't good enough for them!"

Mom, back from the school open house, comes into the room smiling and unbuttoning her coat. "It went well. Really well. We had more parental attendance than in any of the last five years!" She stops and sees Dad's wild-eyed look. "What's wrong?"

"Sit down," he commands. "Forget about that damn school and other people's kids for a minute, and sit down! We've got something to tell you."

Mom sits stiffly on the edge of the couch, coat still on. "What is this?" The lighthearted tone is gone and she looks from Dad to me.

"I'll tell you what this is," Dad bellows, standing firmly in front of her, hands on hips. "Everything Adrienne told us is true. Did you hear me, Helen? It's true!"

Mom's face turns white, and in a small voice she says, "It can't be."

"It is! I heard it from your little daughter—*from our three-year-old!* Word for word, only worse than Adri ever said. She described everything—things she could not possibly know if she hadn't experienced them! *Now* try to deny it happened!"

"Mark, don't!" Mom throws her hands over her face and backs away.

"Wake up! Take your head out of the sand! It's been going on for years, and we keep finding explanations so we don't have to face the truth!"

"Adrienne!" Mom cries, "what have you been telling your sister? What kind of ideas have you put in her head?"

"Mom, I didn't!"

Dad moves to my chair and puts a hand on my head. "Don't you dare blame her. We're both to blame. We didn't see what was right in front of our eyes. We were so *naive*—so ready to accept things at their face value—while that witch . . ."

"I can't believe it!" Mom says in a whisper.

"No? Then listen to this tape. Listen! Adrienne knew we'd never believe her so she had the foresight to tape what Becky said. Adrienne, play it for her!"

"No!" Mom backs away as if someone is about to strike her.

"Yes! You'll never believe it for sure if you don't hear for yourself. Play it, Adrienne!"

Reluctantly, eyes on Mom, I go to the tape recorder and reverse the tape. For a few moments the only sounds in the room are those of the tape rushing backwards. Then I push the button and the tape starts forward again. There is Brown Bear's voice, and then Becky's . . .

133

"That's enough! Enough!" Mom cries. "Turn it off!" She jumps out of her seat and runs to the recorder to click it off, then bursts out crying.

"Mom . . . don't . . ." I say, putting my arms around her. "Please, Mom . . . don't . . ."

She sobs against my shoulder, mumbling apologies.

Dad comes up behind us and throws his arms around both of us. "I'm sorry . . . I'm sorry . . . Come. Sit down. Let's figure out what to do about all this."

When Mom calms down and wipes her eyes, she takes my hand and just shakes her head. She doesn't need to speak. I can feel the depth of her regret and sorrow. For the first time in so very many years I feel a small link with her.

"Okay. What do we do now? Call the police? Get all the preschool parents together and tell them what we know? Yes. That's the first thing to do. And tomorrow Becky stays home. Either I'll take her into the office or you call in absent. Now, who else do you know has kids in Treehouse?"

Mom names one or two people she knows, and we look up their phone numbers in the directory. Though it's after nine at night, Dad makes the calls. He introduces himself and says, "I wonder if you could both come over to our home this evening, say in an hour? If not both of you, at least one. It's very important. It has to do with the possibility of child abuse at Treeschool." Nobody declines, and with each call he makes he learns the names of a few other families until he has reached a dozen or more.

While he's calling, Mom is moving around mechanically, organizing refreshments. I help get out cups and saucers, while Mom throws together a simple coffee cake from a box mix and puts it in the microwave. Lips tight and brow wrinkled, she leans against the counter, both hands on the tile as if she hasn't the strength to undergo the next few hours.

Almost twenty parents arrive. It's late, ten o'clock, but the seriousness of Dad's call has brought them out, nevertheless.

"Do I have to be here?" I ask Dad before the first of them comes. He understands how embarrassing it will be for me to relate such intimate things to total strangers, though I know now that if the police become involved, I'll have no choice.

"No, darling. Your tape should be convincing enough. Becky explained everything as she showed what was done to her."

I listen nearby. Dad's revelations shock everyone and there are cries of "Ridiculous!" and "Impossible!" "Treehouse is one of the finest schools in the state. I'd never have sent my child there otherwise!" one mother cries. "Don't you think we'd have known if something like that was going on?"

And then Daddy plays the tape.

There is shock, of course, and denial. "Maybe it happened to your child, but it couldn't have happened to mine!"

Yet even as there are denials, I can see from my view

into the living room that some people say nothing, and that even some of those who deny are beginning to think.

"I took my son to the doctor. He had bleeding from the rectum," a woman relates slowly, choosing her words as if she was walking on a path of broken glass. "The doctor said it was due to . . . constipation."

"My daughter has been crying every time I take her to school lately."

". . . redness . . ."

". . . vaginal infections . . ."

". . . nightmares . . ."

All the things that happened to Becky, and more.

By the time they leave, close to midnight, there is agreement that the police must be informed immediately. Denial and disbelief have been replaced by tears and rage.

The story isn't over yet. It won't be for years, perhaps. Martha Plunkett denies vehemently that anything like child abuse went on at her school. She insists it's all circumstantial, that the ideas were all put in Becky's head by me, that I'm a pathological liar or a psychopath. And that the other parents are reading things into perfectly innocent acts. Many people believe her because she *seems* so reliable. After all, she's been running Treehouse for nineteen years.

Meanwhile, the police are investigating. They're talking to all the parents. The children who were students are seeing special child psychologists, and the psychologists report that through puppets and dolls they're hearing terrible stories of abuse by strangers as well as Treehouse teachers and aides. Soon they're going to check out the kids who went to Treehouse years ago, like me.

The psychologists say that Treehouse isn't typical. And everybody else says that most preschools are wonderful, rich experiences for kids.

I guess, too, that one good thing came out of all this. My parents say they're going to listen better, not just *hear*, but listen. And not just to what we say, but to *what we don't say*.

"I really didn't believe it," Bev confides to me when the whole thing breaks. (She and Jason are cooling it for a while. She says she "isn't ready" for a closer relationship, but she's hurting because she really misses him.) "It's so horrible. . . . Are you seeing the therapist, that Dr. Shapiro?"

I *have* started seeing her and it's helping. We're sifting through all the years that I couldn't remember. And she's making me understand that I'm not to blame and that I don't have to be perfect to be loved, and that I *can* say No. It's my body and my right. Becky is going to a therapist too and she'll probably testify at the trial coming up against Plunkett and the other Treehouse teachers.

Ryan and I are seeing each other again.

At first I was scared that he'd not be able to put out of his mind these dirty pictures of me as an abused baby. But the first time we talk it's as if nothing ever happened.

I test him. "So, how does it feel being seen with a former Miss Porno Pinup?" I ask, waiting breathlessly for his answer to my putdown.

"Quit it, Adri. I don't think of you that way. And you should know that. Now, how about going to the roller rink Saturday?"

"Are you sure you want to?"

"No. I just like to ask in hopes you'll refuse."

"I can't promise anything."

He sighs a deep, long-suffering sigh. "Let's not go through that again, woman!"

And I smile. I think it will be all right now. Or in time, anyway. I think, when he kisses me one day soon I'll be able to kiss him back the way I want to, the way I've always wanted to. And it will be as wonderful as Bev says.

Child Sexual Assault

It is illegal for adults or older children to have sexual intercourse or any kind of sexual intimacy with children. If you have been sexually assaulted in this way or if you are being assaulted now, try to talk to someone you trust – perhaps your parents, your teacher or your doctor. If you have no one you can talk to, contact the organisations listed here. They will believe you and will help you. It is vital that you seek this help.

Childline
Freepost 1111 (no stamp needed)
London EC4 4BB
phone number 088 1111 (the number is the same wherever you live: it is a freephone (just dial without putting any money in); the service is open 24 hrs)

The Social Services
The number of your local social services office will be in the phone book.

The National Society for the Prevention of Cruelty to Children (NSPCC)
(branches in England, Wales and Northern Ireland)
67 Saffron Hill,
London EC1N 8RS
(01) 242 1626

Royal Scottish Society for the Prevention of Cruelty to Children
Melville House,
41 Poleworth Terrace,
Edinburgh EH11 1NU
(031) 337 8539/8530

Australia
Sydney
Child Protection and Family Crisis – (02) 818 5555
(24 hours)
2UE Kids Careline – (02) 929 7799 (9 am to 5 pm, Mon–Fri)
Darwin
Department for Community Development – (089) 814 733
Brisbane
Crisis Care – (07) 224 6855 (24 hours)
Adelaide
Crisis Care – (08) 272 1222 (24 hours)
Hobart
Department of Community Welfare, Crisis Intervention
(002) 302 529 (24 hours)
Melbourne
Protective Services for Children – (03) 309 5700 (9 am to 5 pm)
Perth
Crisis Care – (09) 321 4144 (24 hours) or (008) 199 008 (toll free)

You can also contact through your local directory:
The Police
Lifeline
Rape Crisis Centres

New Zealand
Auckland
Help – 399 185 (24 hours)

I Never Loved Your Mind

Paul Zindel

'Look, Dewey-Smewey whateverthehellyournameis. Don't put me in the same class with you. You come off like a lazy spoiled punk whose Momsy and Popsy think they're committing some type of middle-class progressiveness by letting you drop out of school because you bellyached too much. I think you're just one more of our sick society's ridiculous, dangerous wastes. That's what I think.'

So Yvette, idealist, vegetarian, burdened by her concern for society's evils, takes a verbal swipe at Dewey, clever, curious and friendly. But he catches her out, and gradually they realise that perhaps they do have something in common.

'Highly topical, this is a crazily funny and crazily moving love (or non-love) story between a boy and girl around 17 or 18, in the Holden Caulfield line. Clever stuff.'
Observer

The Pigman, *My Darling, My Hamburger*, and *Pardon Me, You're Stepping on My Eyeball!* are also in Lions Tracks.

A Sound of Chariots

Mollie Hunter

Bridie McShane grew up in a village in the Lowlands of
Scotland after World War I, the noisiest, most spirited
and also the most sensitive of five children. Her father, a
veteran of the war, died when she was nine, and Bridie
was shattered by grief. She was also possessed by the
consciousness of time passing and the reality of her own
eventual death, and haunted by the sound of 'Time's
winged chariot hurrying near'. But Bridie was a gifted
child, and gradually she was able to come to terms with
her grief through her desire to be a writer.

'This moving story, told with deliberate simplicity, is shot
through with tenderness and insight.' *Glasgow Herald*

'An exceptional book which shines light on the clouds of
glory without dispelling them.' *Sunday Telegraph*

'Tough, yet tender, humorous, yet tragic, sometimes
horrific yet always compassionate.'
Times Literary Supplement

LIONS · TRACKS

A Question of Courage

Marjorie Darke

Em could hardly credit her own daring – here she was, Emily Palmer from the back streets of Birmingham, carrying a placard that boldly read VOTES FOR WOMEN in a bicycle parade, and on a Sunday too! But Em had been swept into the cause by the eloquent Louise Marshall, and though their lives were worlds apart, Emily knew she'd had enough of being a 'bloomin' slave'. Already she'd spent five years sewing for a pittance and she was only eighteen.

The night that Emily and Louise were caught red-handed painting slogans on the golf course sealed both their friendship and their fight. Then came London and Mrs Pankhurst's Suffragette Movement, and the cloak and dagger fun was over. Now it was rallies, imprisonment, and most terrible of all, force feeding. But as the movement and its violence grew, so did Emily's self-doubts, and for her the choice of continuing the fight became a question of courage.

LIONS · TRACKS

It's My Life

Robert Leeson

"You're playing hard to get," Sharon had said as Jan walked off, away from school and from Peter Carey's invitation to the college disco on Friday night. Was she? Jan didn't really know. She wanted time to think things out, ask Mum what she thought.

But when Mum doesn't come home, Jan finds her own problems taking second place, as she is expected to cope with running the house for her father and younger brother Kevin, as well as studying for exams and trying to sort out her feelings towards Peter. Slowly she realises what sort of life her mother led, the loneliness and the pressures she faced, and with this realisation comes Jan's firm resolve that despite the expectations of family, neighbours and friends, she will decide things for herself; after all, "It's my life."